BLAZING
UNCANNY
TRAILS

For my grandfather, who loves Westerns but really dislikes the supernatural crap.

Except for the Lizard Man.

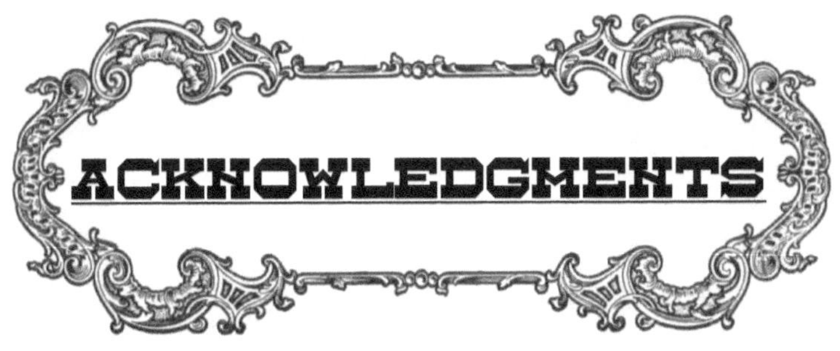


Most of these stories were first published by small publishers willing to give a new writer a chance.

Thank you all.

A special thank you to David Boop and David Riley for their encouragement, support, and indoctrination into the Weird West.

And thank you to Rhye Manhattan for allowing the inclusion of *Moshito Masquine* into this collection.

# New Mexico Territory

# 1850

Swoop Smith wiped at the gritty dirt in his eyes. Mining above his head was turning out to be more of a chore than he had expected, but he was following a gold vein that seemed to be widening, and he wasn't about to quit. He was on the verge of being a rich man.

The small tunnel that had taken him all summer to carve out with his shovel and pickaxe extended nearly twenty-five feet into the side of the rocky hill, but was little wider his own shoulders. He was having difficulty swinging the pick in the tight space, but now that he had found good color, he was loathe to waste effort on widening it.

He struck at the stone above his head again and again, fighting the cramped space. The metal head of the pick sang between blows, filling the tunnel with sounds. A glancing blow tossed a shower of sparks at his face, and a piece of hot rock hit his eye.

"Goddamn!" Swoop dropped the axe and put his hands to his face. He knew better than to rub, he had scratched his eyes before, so instead he just pressed. His eye watered, but the rock didn't come out.

Hand still covering his injury, Swoop headed out of the tunnel, leaving his tools and lantern behind. The glow of day was not far away in the short tunnel, and he had no problem feeling his way back.

Squinting his good eye in the bright sun of the arid desert, he headed for his makeshift camp; a bedroll and supplies piled up just outside the mine entrance. His sudden appearance from the mine must have startled his horses, as they both reared and pulled against their tethers. He ignored them as he fumbled with a waterskin and poured water into his eye.

He looked up into the clear, blue sky, blinking rapidly, trying to clear his vision and hoping he hadn't done any permanent damage.

The horses were still acting up. "Settle down!" His voice was strong, yet calm. He took a drink of water before pouring more over his eye.

A boulder shifted up on the hill behind him, and loose rocks fell around his feet.

Swoop spun around and stumbled away from the hill, afraid of being hit by falling rock. His vision, fouled with the water, failed him as he watched for signs of a landslide. He wiped at his eyes with his sleeves, trying to see through the blur. His heart jumped as he realized the horses likely hadn't been spooked by him.

"Who's there?" He suspected a cougar, but he made no sudden movements. He didn't want to get shot going for his rifle if it was a man.

No reply came.

He waited for his eyes to clear. He thought someone had been poking around his camp the last couple of days, but he had seen no sign other than a few things out of place. A white man would have revealed himself or stolen everything by now, so he suspected an Indian. The local tribes were Hopi and Navajo, and the Navajo were not known for being friendly.

The horses were finally settling down, and Swoop's eyes cleared enough he was sure there was no one on the hill above him. He wiped at his eyes and looked one more time. There was no one there. That convinced him it was either an animal or an Indian. He would like to think was just a rockslide, but the horses wouldn't have reacted that way if nothing had been there.

He took another swig from his waterskin and casually tossed it back, doing his best to seem unconcerned. He hoped if he didn't appear threatening, he would be able to make it back into his mine and grab his rifle.

As he turned for the tunnel, something on the ground caught his eye. A track.

So he did have a visitor after all. The track seemed odd, but he didn't want to stop to investigate until he had a rifle in his hand.

The tunnel was pitch black compared to the full daylight, and Swoop had a more difficult time working his way back in than he'd had coming out. Even when he made it back to the area illuminated by his lantern, his sight was too dim to see well. He grabbed his rifle from where it leaned against the wall and headed right back out.

He slowed when he could see out of the mine and into the day, assessing the situation. The horses were calm now, but they both kept their ears cocked towards the area the rocks had fallen from. Swoop slowly entered into the daylight again, keeping watch for any movement.

Making his way to the track he had seen, he kneeled to get a good look at it. It was nearly the length of his own footprint, but it had three toes that splayed twice as wide as his boot. It put Swoop in mind of a giant turkey track.

Standing up, he looked around for more tracks. He didn't see any. A flying bird would put into account his not finding tracks before, too. An old Indian legend of the Thunderbird came to his mind, and Swoop was sure a bird with a foot that size could carry off children. No wonder the horses had been nervous.

No longer worried about getting shot by another human, Swoop checked his supplies. As before, things mostly looked like he had left them, and he probably wouldn't have noticed anything had been touched, except this time something was missing. His salt.

His whole pouch had been dug out of his food and taken. And everything else had been put back.

A chill ran down Swoop's spine. Animals don't put things back.

Swoop moved away from his supplies as a feeling of unease settled over him. He glanced at the horses. They were calm, but were still focused on the hillside above him.

Rifle in hand, Swoop went to them and stroked each gently across the nose as he looked back up the hill where they watched. With his eyes, Swoop followed the cut on the hill left by the gravel that had fallen and spotted the boulder that had shifted. Next to the boulder lay a small, worn leather pouch. His salt.

He hefted his rifle to his shoulder and looked for the best way up the hill, finally deciding to circle to the right before coming back across to avoid the loose scree. Keeping watch for any sign of movement above, Swoop had little trouble reaching his pouch, but as he reached down to pick it up, he froze.

Prickles ran up and down his skin and his knees felt weak with fear as he realized his pouch was still clutched in the fingers of ... a hand?

The slender four-fingered hand was the same dusty color and mottled texture of the loose rocks and dirt around it, camouflaging it very well.

As his eyes made out the contours of the hand, he was able to find the forearm and follow the thin shape up, past an elbow, and to the body. And then the head.

Swoop's mouth was dry, and he found he couldn't swallow as he realized the rock next to his foot had closed eyes and nostril slits.

Now that he could see it, the body was obvious. It looked like a small, willowy man, with the head of a lizard.

As he examined the form, he realized the real boulder had crushed a leg. He could see the dark of the blood soaked into the dirt around the edge of the large rock.

The creature wasn't moving, but Swoop decided to take no chances. He raised his rifle and aimed for the middle of the skull. As his finger tightened on the trigger, he realized the beast wore something around its neck.

He lowered the rifle and peered closer. A collar? Could this creature belong to someone? The material was obviously fabricated. It was an intricate weave of grasses that formed a repeating diamond-shaped pattern.

One of the eyes blinked.

Swoop jumped, and tripped backwards.

The creature woke up and tried to scramble away, but its trapped leg held it pinned. With an eerie hissing, it began flopping and twisting, coiling about itself in an inhuman way, trying to free the leg.

Horrified, Swoop continued backing away. He had seen snakes twist like that, curling and knotting themselves to escape when a boot or a shovel had come down upon their head.

The lizard-thing stopped writhing and froze, staring at Swoop, unblinking. A small forked tongue, black as any serpent's, darted in and out from between inflexible lips. Slowly, the tongue extended out, tasting the air, moving about like a tiny two-fingered arm feeling around for something.

Golden, slitted eyes turned and focused on the salt pouch.

The creature slowly unwound itself, gaze flicking between the pouch and Swoop. When it was untangled, it reached out and picked up the pouch with its four-fingered hand. It brought the pouch close to its face and peered inside, then, using two hands, it pulled the strings and sealed it tightly.

Looking up to Swoop, the lizard man deliberately tossed the pouch to him and waited, watching.

Swoop feared he might vomit. This thing was no creature, no animal. It had intelligence. Had he believed in demons and devils, he would have known this to be one, but Swoop was a man of the earth, and he knew flesh and blood when he saw it.

He bent down and picked up the salt pouch.

The other watched him intently.

When Swoop made no other motion, the reptilian creature slowly closed its eyes and let out a soft hiss, laying its head on the ground. The four fingered hands curled into fists and it pulled its arms in close to its body.

Not knowing what to do, Swoop sat down and watched. The returning of the salt left no doubt in his mind this creature was intelligent. If this were dog, or a horse, he would put it out of its misery. If it were a man, he would help it. But it was neither.

Swoop made his decision and stood up. The golden eyes opened and watched him. Swoop laid his rifle and the salt pouch down and held his hands wide, fingers spread, hoping the creature would recognize he intended no harm.

He approached slowly, trying not to make any threatening moves. For its part, the lizard man watched, but did not move.

Swoop came within reach of the spindly arms and hesitated, ready to spring back, but no hissing or swiping came at him. He kneeled down close to the leg pinned by the boulder and heard a nervous hiss, but there was still no movement.

The boulder couldn't weigh more than a couple of hundred pounds, and the leg was pinned under the edge, so Swoop thought he would have little trouble moving it. He just had to figure out how to do it without hurting the leg more.

He stepped back to where he could meet the lizard man's eyes and made gestures that he hoped would be understood that he was leaving, but would be back. The slitted eyes closed without any sign of acknowledgment or recognition.

Swoop returned with a shovel, an axe, a waterskin, and some jerky. He sat down in front of the lizard man and uncorked his waterskin as the creature watched him. He took a drink, re-corked the skin, and sat it where the thin reptilian arms could reach it. Swoop then took a bite of jerky and made of show of chewing it up before laying the rest of it on top of the waterskin. The golden eyes flicked back and forth between Swoop and his offering, but the creature still did not move.

Not knowing how to reassure a lizard, Swoop got up, grabbed his shovel, and set about freeing the creature's leg. He worked slowly and methodically, being careful not to touch the injured leg or allow the boulder to put more pressure on it. He dug enough room to place a rock to use as a fulcrum and then began using his shovel handle as a lever. When he was ready, he tried to caution the lizard man to prepare, but he still got no response.

He waved his hand to get its attention and it focused on him again. He held up a finger and said "One." He held up another and said "Two." With the third finger and the word "Three," Swoop mimed grunting and pushing the rock off the leg.

The reptilian eyes didn't blink.

Swoop and the creature looked at each other for a moment before the creature tiredly closed its eyes again.

Swoop went back to the boulder. He leveraged his shovel handle and counted out loud. "One. Two. Three!" He pushed down on the handle and the boulder rocked off the lizard man's leg.

The lizard man scrambled away with lightning speed, startling Swoop as the boulder rolled over and began a lumbering roll down the hill. Swoop forgot about the lizard man as he realized his horses might be in danger.

"Hya!" Swoop yelled to get the horses' attention. "Hya!" If they didn't pull off their tethers, he hoped they would at least be able to move out of the way.

He needn't have worried. The rock fell past his mine entrance, hit the ground, and stopped where it landed. The horses were shook up, but they would be fine.

Swoop remembered the lizard man and turned quickly, worried that he had left his back unguarded from attack.

The creature was between him and his rifle. It would have been on all-fours, but for the injured back leg that hung limply. It no longer seemed drowsy. It was completely alert, and it was injured.

Knowing that an injured animal, or man for that matter, was dangerous, Swoop squatted where he was and waited. The lizard man just watched him.

After a moment, Swoop realized the water and jerky were within his reach, so he slowly picked them up and repeated his earlier show of taking a drink and eating. Mouth full, he gently tossed the waterskin toward the lizard man, and followed it with the jerky. Chewing, he waited.

The forked tongue flickered towards the items, writhing in the air, as though it had a life of its own and wanted the food even though the rest of body refused to move. Finally, the golden eyes dropped from Swoop to the waterskin and the creature slowly crept a step forward to reach it.

Swoop was careful not to move as he watched the lizard man sit down. Inhuman hands easily uncorked the waterskin and poured liquid into the gaping reptilian maw. Needle sharp teeth glinted in the sunlight as the water splashed across them. The lizard man capped the skin and tossed it back to Swoop. It picked up the last of the jerky and put it in its mouth. It didn't chew as Swoop had. Instead it worked its long tongue in and out of its mouth as it extended and contracted its neck.

Swoop thought he could see the lump of food moving down as the lizard man showed the smooth pale scales of its throat.

They sat and watched each other for a long time. Swoop was sure there were thoughts in that oblong scaly head, but he was equally sure they were nothing like his, and likely never would be. He doubted they would ever be able to comprehend each other.

The lizard man cocked its head sideways and looked at Swoops rifle.

Swoop felt his belly knot. Would that thing know how to use his rifle? Would it use the rifle if it knew how?

Long thin brown fingers reached out towards the rifle and Swoop tensed, not knowing if he should run towards the creature or away, but knowing he wouldn't be able to get up from his sitting position fast enough.

The fingers stopped short of the rifle, and picked up the salt pouch. Golden eyes turned back to Swoop. The lizard man made some quick, complicated gestures, then, in a move that would have broken a man's back, lowered its head and put its chin on the ground.

It rose back up, and tossed the pouch to Swoop.

Swoop caught the pouch out of the air. When he looked back, the lizard man was gone.

Swoop didn't sleep well the next few nights. His dreams were haunted by lightning quick snakes and lizards that stared at him with intelligent eyes. He had considered leaving his mine, but he was so close to the gold, be couldn't bring himself to.

He continued working the growing vein of gold, making progress inches at a time in the lamp-lit gloom. He had dug out enough to make up for all of the supplies he had bought to get this far, but he was nowhere close to being a rich man yet.

On the fourth day after he had seen the lizard man, an occurrence he was nearly ready to chalk up to hallucinations from being alone for too long, he came out of the cave to find his supplies had been gone through again. This time it was a mess.

"Damn it!" He started toward the pile of supplies.

A hissing sound stopped him in his tracks.

Swoop turned to find the lizard man standing upright on the injured leg. Scabs covered the scaly skin, but the leg appeared strong.

The horses seemed to notice it for the first time and began whinnying and shying away.

It hissed again, looking Swoop in the eye, before it slowly sank into what might be considered a sitting position. It cocked its head and waited.

Swoop imitated it and sank down to sit facing it.

The lizard man held out one of its slender fingered hands and revealed it had the salt pouch. It leaned forward in its impossible way and touched its chin to the ground. Sitting back up, it tossed the pouch to Swoop.

Swoop opened the pouch and looked inside. All of the salt appeared to be there.

Hissing and complex hand gestures from the lizard man were followed by the presentation of another pouch, this one woven from grass, the same as the collar it wore. It tossed the pouch to Swoop.

Swoop caught it out of the air and was surprised by its weight. He pulled at the drawstrings to reveal the contents. Shaking the nugget out into his hand, Swoop could hardly believe his eyes. Gold. Enough to buy a farm.

He felt a stupid grin involuntarily crawling across his face and did his best to suppress it. He looked up at the lizard man.

The slender creature pointed to the salt, then to the gold, then made a gesture of tapping a fist against the flat of its other hand.

"You want to trade?"

The lizard man repeated the motion and waited.

Swoop picked up the salt and tossed it back to the lizard man. He tapped a fist against the palm of his hand. "Trade."

The lizard man hissed in a way Swoop assumed was satisfaction. It rose and turned to leave.

"Wait," Swoop stood.

The smaller figure turned and looked back, cocking its head again.

"Trade more." Swoop made the fist-motion again and followed it with a sweeping gesture.

The lizard man did not appear to understand, so Swoop motioned it to come closer. It stayed where it was.

Swoop proceeded to try to explain. He sat his gold nugget next to the boulder that had fallen from the hill when he had leveraged it off the lizard man's leg. With hand motions, he tried to show that the nugget was little and the boulder was big. Then he pointed to the salt pouch and to the gold and tried to explain that he could trade much more salt for much more gold.

When the lizard man's eyes widened, Swoop knew it had finally understood.

Pointing to the sun, Swoop motioned it moving across the sky and counted. "One." He swept his arm across the sky again. "Two." He continued until he reached seven days. Then he made the trade sign again and pointed to the salt and the gold and motioned for much bigger.

The lizard man watched it all with intent interest and then matched Swoop's hand sign. *Trade.*

<br>

The trip into town took three days.

When Swoop cashed the gold nugget in at the bank, he couldn't keep the grin off his face. He stabled his horses and headed for the hotel and a hot bath. He had never had so much money in his life. It was hard to keep his mouth shut, to not brag, not get drunk and spend the evening with the ladies, but he had his eye on the prize and there would be plenty of time for all of that later.

After a good night's sleep, he bought a wagon and another horse, as neither of his were accustomed to being hitched. He didn't sell either of his horses, thinking perhaps he would buy a ranch, and he might need them.

He restocked his supplies at the general store, buying out all the salt they would sell him. The proprietor had two and a half fifty-pound kegs, but refused to let some crazy fool buy all of the town's supply, so Swoop settled for one and a half kegs.

Swoop was on his way back to his mine before lunch.

The return trip seemed interminable, but Swoop arrived when he expected to; the day before the meeting for the trade.

He didn't bother unloading his wagon, other than the salt kegs. If this trade with the lizard man went as he hoped it would, he would not be staying and digging in his cramped little tunnel anymore.

Swoop had a hard time falling asleep. He no longer had nightmares of lighting quick lizards and snakes, instead, he felt anxious excitement at the thought of meeting the lizard man again. When he awoke at first light, he was surprised he had slept at all.

He set up the salt kegs in the place he had traded with the lizard man before and got ready to settle in and wait. The last thing he expected was the sound of the hammer on a revolver being cocked behind him.

"Hands where I can see them." The voice was full of arrogant self-confidence.

Swoop didn't own a revolver, only his rifle. And he had left that in the wagon so he wouldn't present a threat to the lizard man. He held his hands out to his sides and turned around slowly.

The man's bearded face was unfamiliar, as were two of the three faces of the other men behind him. The last man, though, Swoop recognized. He had been the teller at the bank, where Swoop had cashed in the gold nugget. All of them held guns at the ready.

"Told you boys he'd have a mine out here somewhere," the first man said over his shoulder. He looked back to Swoop. "A man don't buy a wagon and horse with a gold nugget unless he's going back for more."

"Paul," the bearded man looked back again. "You can go get the horses now. He's the only one here."

"Sure thing, Marvin." A gaunt faced man nodded, holstered his gun, and headed around the hill.

"Matthew, you and Pearl check the camp out; see if he's got anything else worth a spit." The other two men headed for Swoop's wagon.

Marvin waved his revolver toward the mine entrance. "Show me where the good stuff is, and you might just come out of this alive."

Swoop turned and looked back at the mine entrance. "We need to get a lantern out of the wagon. It's too dark to see in there without one."

"Pearl! Grab a lantern!" Marvin pointed at the mine again. "Get moving."

Beyond the hill, a horse screamed, and the sound of hooves grew loud.

Marvin turned to look and Swoop went for his gun. Swoop was too slow and Marvin was ready. The bearded man smashed the flat of the gun's grip across Swoop's face, breaking his nose and blinding him with pain. Swoop fell to his knees.

"You try that again, and I'll kill you on the spot!" Marvin kicked him, knocking him down.

As his vision cleared, Swoop saw four horses sprinting past in a panic.

"Paul!" Marvin called out but there was no answer. "Matthew! Pearl! Go check on Paul!"

A strangled cry sounded from by the wagon. Swoop looked just in time to see a brown flash of movement disappear behind some brush. Matthew waivered on his feet for a moment holding his throat, then fell face-first into the dirt.

Pearl screamed and waved his gun wildly. "What the hell was that! Marvin! Something is out here!"

Marvin fired a shot at the brush Swoop had seen the lizard man vanish into.

"What the hell was that, Marvin? It killed Matthew!" Pearl's voice was high and shaky.

"Indians!" Marvin yelled as he turned, scanning the hill above them. "Get down!"

"That wasn't no goddamned Indian! It wasn't no …!" Pearl fell silent.

Swoop, holding his bloody nose, looked back to Pearl, but the man was gone.

Marvin whipped the tip of his revolver back and forth, pointing where Pearl had been. "What the hell…?"

Swoop blinked and a slender brown figure appeared behind Marvin. With a move so fast Swoop couldn't follow, the lizard man raked his claws across Marvin's throat and ran back behind some rocks.

Marvin spun around to face an attacker that was no longer there, his mouth working, but no sound coming out. He dropped his gun and put both hands to his neck. His eyes met Swoop's, pleading, as he fell to his knees.

Swoop moved out of the way as Marvin's body fell to the ground.

Using one of the salt kegs to steady himself, Swoop stood up and wiped blood from his eyes.

The lizard man hesitantly walked out from behind a pile of rocks, scabs still evident on its leg. It cocked its head and looked at Swoop.

Swoop held his arms wide, fingers spread, and then sat back down.

The lizard man sat down and looked at him expectantly.

Pulling one of the kegs close, Swoop opened it, reached in and pulled out a handful of salt. He let the white grains fall between his fingers and back into the keg.

The lizard man's tongue snaked out, groping at the air, tasting for the salt.

Swoop replaced the lid and pushed the keg toward the lizard man. He then pushed the second keg forward and made the fist-palm sign for trade.

The lizard man hissed, and a movement behind Swoop startled him. He turned to see five lizard men walking forward, each carrying two heavy bags made of animal skin.

It was disconcerting to be surrounded by the lizard men, but after what he had seen them do to Marvin and his men, Swoop knew if they had intended him harm he couldn't have stopped them.

The bags were set in front of Swoop and opened up. One of the lizard men reached into a bag and lifted a handful of gold nuggets, allowing them to slip through its four-fingered hand and back into the bag.

*Trade.* The lizard man sitting across from Swoop signaled.

*Trade,* Swoop signaled back.

Excitement among the other lizard men became immediately evident as they moved around the salt kegs with uncanny speed, hissing at each other.

*More Trade?* The first lizard man signaled to Swoop.

*More Trade,* he answered.

The lizard man began drawing the sun in the dirt and marking days. Another symbol soon became clear to be the moon, and Swoop realized the lizard man was asking for a trade in the spring.

*In the spring, more trade. Salt. Gold.* Swoop answered.

The lizard man seemed pleased. It stood up and hissed. One of the other lizard men brought over a small pouch and left again. The lizard man with the scabs on its leg began gesturing again, and Swoop was hard pressed to follow.

It gestured to the other lizard men and the bodies of Marvin, Pearl, and Matthew. Swoop noticed for the first time that Paul's body had been drug over from wherever he had been killed.

The lizard man tossed Swoop the pouch and Swoop opened it. Inside was the largest uncut diamond he had ever heard of.

*Trade*, motioned the lizard man. *More trade in the spring. Salt. Gold. Diamond. Men. Bring more men.*

## The Dakota Territory

## 1865

Bart looked up from the dusty trail, past the blue uniforms of the men marching ahead of him, and out into to the prairie wasteland to see what had set the rest of the cavalry muttering. Anything would be a welcome distraction from all of the goddamned marching. He hadn't signed up for the cavalry to *walk* across the country. It's the cavalry, for God's sake! He was supposed to be on a damned horse.

Unable to see what was ahead, nor catch what was being said, Bart huffed disgustedly. Truth be told, he hadn't signed up for the cavalry at all. He'd been sentenced to it. But it was a far sight better'n being hung, which was the other option he'd been given after being court martialed for stealing teeth from the bodies of fallen soldiers to sell to dentists. The only reason he hadn't been shot right then and there was that he'd been caught taking teeth from the bodies of Rebs. It was a damned good thing the men who'd caught him couldn't tell where all of the other teeth in his pouch had come from.

As his part of the column crested a small grassy hill, Bart spotted the unit's scout, a filthy Indian half-breed called Little Big Deer Dick or some other goddamned stupid injun name. Wasn't fair that boot-licker got a horse while everyone else had to walk. The scrawny heathen sat astride a dappled Palomino that, taking into account Bart had once heard California paid twenty-five cents an Indian scalp, was worth a thousand times more than the red-skinned sneak-thief.

The scout waved a hand sharply through the air, gesturing as he talked to Lieutenant Blackwell.

No, he wasn't talking to the lieutenant—he was arguing. Bart raised his eyebrows as he unconsciously went up on his toes to try to see better. Watching this dumb injun worrying at his own grave was the most interesting thing that had happened since Wilton had almost shit on a rattlesnake three days ago.

A wry grin split Bart's dirty face, revealing the other reason Bart had been collecting dead men's teeth: his own yellow and brown teeth that had been cracked and broken by the butt of a rifle in the Battle of Pine Bluff, and he'd hoped a dentist would fix them in trade for more teeth.

The column came to an abrupt halt, and Bart almost ran into Matthews' back. Leaning out to see around the others, he saw the supply wagon pull out of formation as Sergeant Prescott, who was driving it, angled closer to be part of the discussion with the Scout.

"Ten dollars says Blackwell shoots the injun." Whitey's cracked voice whispered from behind Bart, loud enough for men to hear several rows away.

"I'll take that bet!"

"I'm in."

"God, I hope so. That'd be one more horse we could take turns on."

"Oh, *now* you're feeling sorry 'bout all those horses we was ordered to shoot back in Kentucky to slow down Johnny Reb. Bit late for regrets, now that we're walkin' all the way t' hell."

"I just don't understand why we have to go get the damn horses. They could have brought the horses to us."

Voices all around answered in dry, hoarse whispers of agreement and wager. Bart ignored them and kept watching. He didn't want to miss the show. After a week of marching across the plains of Dakota, anything bigger than a buzzing fly was entertainment.

The half-breed scout made a wide gesture with his arm, pointing all around ahead of the column of men, then he raised his finger higher. Bart followed the gesture to the giant thunder clouds looming in the western sky. Lightning flickered sideways across the sky, out across one cloud and disappearing into the belly of the next, like a rodent running from hole to hole.

Bart blew through his lips, making a flatulent sound. It would be a miserable night in a leaky tent. Assuming he was one of the men who got a tent.

Lieutenant Blackwell shouted at the scout and pointed vigorously at the red-skinned runt and then to the west. The tone of Blackwell's voice made Bart smile again, even if he couldn't catch the words.

The Indian's back stiffened and he went still upon his horse, staring at the lieutenant.

"Oh, shit! He's in for it now!" Ryan giggled from up ahead, glancing back and showing his toothless smile. Bart had no use for Ryan. His constant sniveling and nervous laughter was enough to gag an outhouse rat. "You don't piss off Blackwell without..."

Ryan fell silent as Lieutenant Blackwell drew his sidearm and pointed it at the scout's head.

Bart's fingers twitched as he watched, holding his breath.

A puff of gunpowder smoke appeared and the scout's head jerked backwards. The body was halfway to the ground before Bart heard the report from the shot.

"Hot damn!" Whitey cried out and slapped his dusty knee with his hat, revealing the long curly white hair he was named for. "I knowed it! Pay up, boys!"

Bart grinned fiercely at the curses of the men around him. He should have bet someone the half-breed was gonna get it. He'd known that worthless piece of crap was—

Movement out in the grass to the side of the column caught his eye. Bart stared hard, trying to spot what had caught his attention.

"Anyone else see that?"

No one answered him. They were too busy passing greasy, crumpled dollar scripts back and forth.

From up ahead, Lieutenant Blackwell, holding the reins of the dead scout's horse, shouted for the column to start moving forward again. Sergeant Prescott pulled the supply wagon in a tight circle around the body and returned to formation. Bart kept his eyes out on the grass where he thought he'd seen something as he started walking again.

In the afternoon heat, the heavy smell of fresh blood made the dust in the air seem thicker and distracted Bart from his concerns as he neared the scout's body. Flies already covered the corpse. Blood splatter coated the brown stalks of grass, and Bart couldn't help but notice how the mud it made stuck to everyone's boots in small clumps.

"Wonder what he did?" Ryan didn't smile this time. He looked from the twisted body to the faces of the other men around him.

"I'd say it was something he didn't do," ventured Whitey. "Looked to me like he refused to follow an order."

"Lookee there!" Someone from behind snorted. "He *didn't* have enough brains to do what he was told!"

"Shit. Weren't nothing that half-breed wouldn't do for a bottle of whiskey."

"You'd know, wouldn'tcha, Stills?"

Laughter broke out around Bart, and, as the column moved past the body, he wondered if anyone could tell a white man's teeth from a red man's. He could make a fortune in California with teeth and scalps. Pulling his eyes away from the dead scout, he looked back to the thunderclouds. Dark and heavy, it hardly seemed possible they could stay up in the air. In the distance, silhouettes of birds rode the air currents, swooping and circling in front of the coming storm. A storm that big made Bart nervous.

He didn't see any smudging of the sky under the clouds to indicate rain yet. That meant the storm might not open up until it was on top of the men, and storms were at their worst when they first broke free. Could be that's what the injun had been worried about.

Bart tried to see ahead of the column, looking for any sign they were marching into a flood plain. The knee-high grasses prevented him from making out what the distant ground was like. This might be a mighty bad place to get caught in a gully-whomper.

Something to the left caught his eye. He kept his gaze focused on the spot as he walked.

Muttering came down the ranks again. Those around Bart strained to hear what the men ahead were saying. With a last nervous glance to his left, Bart gave up watching for movement and turned his attention to the snippets of conversation he could catch.

The words coming back were confusing. He made out "baby" just as the men in front of him came to a halt again.

The wind, pushed out from the oncoming storm, rustled the grass around the soldiers, as though unseen creatures rushed past, darting around their legs. The world filled with the dry, raspy sound now that their heavy boots no longer pounded the grass stalks flat.

Distantly, the unmistakable wail of a lone infant carried across the empty prairie.

Men all around leaned out of formation, trying to see. Bart was bold enough to take a few steps out of line. He paused to use some un-trampled grass to scrape a bloody mud clump from the tip of his boot.

Blackwell shouted something and Bart looked up to see the Lieutenant pointing down into the grass. Three Cavalrymen ran over and grabbed at something on the ground. Two of them came up, struggling to hold an Indian squaw upright as she fought and tried to pull away. The woman was covered with grass, tied into bundles and affixed to her clothes. The third Cavalryman stood up, holding a squalling papoose that was also covered in grass bundles.

"What in the hell...?" Whitey's hoarse voice hissed next to Bart. "Looks like Sioux."

"Lakota," came a reply from someone ahead.

Bart spit. "Who gives a—"

"Injuns!" Someone from behind hollered. "It's a trap!"

Bart reflexively looked to the sound of the voice. Men all around him were unshouldering rifles and dropping to take aim at clumps of grass that seemed to move against the tug of the wind.

Bart dropped all the way down into the tall grass, hiding his head as he fumbled with his own rifle. Whitey fell next to him, and Bart could hear other men around them drop and roll away, spreading out and seeking better cover.

"I don't see anything," Whitey hissed. "You?"

"I don't know which way to look." Bart hissed, but he wasn't about to put his head up and get it shot off. He squirmed in the dirt, turning around and facing toward the front of the column.

A peal of thunder echoed across the plains, and, at first, Bart thought someone had fired their rifle.

"Sergeant says they're hiding in the grass all around us! Pass it on!" The warning came down the column. Whitey repeated it, but his harsh voice didn't carry.

"Pass it on, Bart!" Whitey yelled at him.

Bart grimaced. He sure as shit didn't want to be giving away his position. Ryan beat him to it.

"Sergeant says they're hiding in the grass all around us! Pass it on!" Ryan's voice was high pitched and nervous. Bart allowed himself a small triumphant smirk. Let that useless bastard give away his position.

"Get back to back with me, Bart." Whitey called as he crawled closer. "You watch forward, I'll watch back. There are enough men behind us I think we'll hear any trouble that way."

Bart grunted in annoyance that Whitey was still trying to give them away, but he twisted his body back around. He still kept his head too low to see over the grass.

Lightning flashed and momentarily brightened the world. Bart glanced up. The clouds had already blocked out the sun and were moving in quick and angry.

A shot rang out just as the thunder rumbled over Bart and Whitey, preventing Bart from being sure which direction the shot had come from.

"Who fired?" Whitey asked.

"I couldn't tell," Bart hissed, wishing Whitey would shut up and leave him alone.

"Shit! Where are they?" Whitey muttered and shifted, lifting himself up to see.

"Keep your fool head down!" Bart hissed at him. "Wanna get us shot?"

"Goddamnit! I need to know where they are!"

A horrible scream came from somewhere toward the head of the column. Bart couldn't tell if it was a man or a woman. He hoped it was that squaw.

"Jesus!" Whitey looked over his shoulder at Bart. "What was that?"

"Someone dying." Bart had heard sounds like that on the battlefield before.

"Jesus!"

Whitey shifted again and began to rise up. Bart kicked at him in frustration. "You tryin' to die? Ain't you been in battle afore?"

A long wailing scream carried through the rising wind. This one, Bart was sure, was from a man. It carried on, pausing only as the lungs that gave it voice refilled to allow it to begin again. The cry faded, but not as Bart was used to when someone died, but rather with distance, like a train whistle moving away.

"God Almighty! It sounds like Lucifer hisself took 'im!" Whitey pushed up onto his knees this time, getting his head high enough to see.

"Get down!" Bart kicked at Whitey.

Whitey froze; his jaw slack, terror etched into his features.

The world flashed dark, as though black lightning had struck out from hell, and a sudden gust of wind pressed Bart's face into the earth. "What the—?"

Whitey was gone.

Goddamn injuns! Bart frantically searched for something, anything in the grass around him. How could they be so damned fast?

An anguished shriek tore the air above him. As chilling as it was terrified, it could never be mistaken for anything but a death knell.

Bart looked up just as a giant black shape circled back, catching the air currents and climbing higher. His mouth went dry as he stared at the bird of prey. It was of ungodly size; a gigantic raptor, with Whitey, still screeching, dangling from its talons, his guts ripped open and his entrails trailing behind him in the air.

Men's voices called out in surprise and shock from all around. Bart wasn't the only one to see it.

Several shots roared and Whitey's screams were mercifully silenced. More shots followed, and Bart was sure men were shooting at the beast, but it showed no sign of noticing, and he couldn't take his eyes off it.

He felt sick. His hands trembled. He knew how to hide during battle, how to avoid soldiers, but how could he hide from death that flew down from the sky?

Unsure what to do, his normal survival strategy useless, Bart began belly crawling through the grass toward the supply wagon. If he could get under the supply wagon, he would be safe there. He kept trying to watch the sky as he furiously moved his knees and elbows, propelling himself forward. He had to get under that wagon, under cover.

One of Bart's elbows stuck deep into a hidden fox's hole. His face hit the dirt as he lost balance. The jolt of pain made him freeze, and he realized he had momentarily lost himself to panic.

Nearly everyone he had ever seen get killed, who hadn't been so foolish as to just walk out into battle standing up, had died because they panicked. He had to stay in control.

A gurgling cry nearby startled him, and he pressed low to the ground. A shape passed by in the thick grass, but he couldn't tell what it was. It was like the grass itself was moving.

It was a goddamned injun.

It must be camouflaged just like that squaw, with grass tied all over. The damned injuns were hiding from the bird.

Bart nodded to himself as he finished reasoning it out.

The bird is what the scout must have known was coming with the storm, why he wouldn't go on.

It would be better to die from a gunshot than at the claws of that bird. But Bart didn't intend either.

He waited until he was as sure as he could be that the Indian had passed by, then began digging at the loose dirt of the fox's hole, widening the opening. How big he could make it, he didn't know, but he would get as much of himself in as he could, and the rest he would cover with dirt and grass. He would wait this out, and he would survive again.

Hell. With a giant bird carrying people away, all he had to do was wait until everyone was gone, and they would have to assume he had died. Then he could walk away from the damned cavalry without anyone chasing after him.

Lightning flashed as he dug. Deafening thunder echoed like Satan's laughter as another high pitched scream went up into the sky.

And then another. Screams scrawled anguish across the heavens in blood.

Bart slowed and risked a glance skyward. Christ Almighty, how many birds were there?

The dark clouds overhead flashed with yellow and white lightning, and in those flashes, Bart saw the birds he had seen from so far away before. They still floated lazily on the air currents, circling and spiraling overhead, but they were enormous, eagle-like, larger than any animal he'd ever laid eyes upon. And there were dozens of them. They were swooping down and snatching men away as easily as an owl takes a mouse.

Bart furiously went back to burying himself. He was nearly finished to his satisfaction when lightning flashed and struck so close the shockwave shook him out of his hole. Nearly blind and deaf, Bart scurried like a drunken rat trying to get back into its den. The green spots in his eyes slowly gave way as he burrowed in again.

Something grabbed his shoulder.

Bart screamed, but a hand clamped over his mouth, silencing him. He fought to break free, but an iron grip held him tight as someone hissed into his ear. Bart couldn't understand the words, but the meaning was clear. He went still.

The hand was removed from Bart's face and an Indian slowly moved into his field of view.

"You're a goddamned big buck, aint'cha?" Bart glanced nervously at the man, searching for weapons.

The Indian put fingers to his lips, indicating Bart should be quiet, and began pulling bushy balls of dried grass from a leather pouch. His movements were slow and deliberate as he held one out to Bart.

"You movin' slow, so the birds don't spot you?"

The Indian frowned and put his fingers to his lips again as he urged Bart to take the grass. He pointed with two fingers to his eyes, then to Bart's blue uniform, and then to the sky.

"You're sayin' the birds can see me."

Another scream echoed across the dark skies, followed by more shots. Bart and the Indian looked up to see another man in a blue uniform being carried away.

When they dropped their gazes, their eyes met. Bart knew he would have to slit the big buck's throat the next time the big injun looked away. He needed the Indian's dirt colored clothes.

The Indian stopped trying to hand Bart the grass and sniffed at the air. Bart slowly slid his hand down to his belt and put his hand on the pommel of his knife. The Indian didn't seem to notice.

Bart leapt, his knife flashing at the Indian's throat. The buck's eyes widened as he turned and intercepted Bart's attack, deflecting the knife away from his neck, but catching the blade across his face, laying open a wide slash from the bridge of his nose to his ear. With a quick move, the Indian tossed Bart to the side.

Bart rolled away, coming up into a crouch, ready to fight or run. He stopped as black smoke washed over him. The ruddy glow of flames climbed above the top of the grass mere feet from him. The crackling of burning grass was loud in his ears, and he could already feel the heat. The lightning had started a prairie fire.

Bart's gut tightened. One of his first jobs with the cavalry was to set a prairie fire in Kansas, to burn out the Indian's hunting ground. He'd never seen the like, as it ate the grasslands in a rage. Hell on Earth, he'd heard others call it, the flames of Perdition itself.

Unless the clouds opened up and dropped Noah's flood on them in the next few minutes, any man caught downwind of the fire was done for.

Bart looked back to the Indian, and cursed when he realized the big buck was gone. God only knew if he would get another opportunity at camouflaged clothes.

Bart gathered up the clumps of grass the Indian had left behind and tried sticking them to his uniform, keeping his attention on the fire. He was downwind, but the fire was still small, not yet the twenty-foot high inferno he knew would come. Thick smoke swirled in and threatened to suffocate him. He had to try and get around the fire. His pulse quickened with anticipation as the flames grew close enough to burn his skin.

Bart gave up on the grass as he could do little other than jam it into his pockets. He jumped up and ran toward the supply wagon. The flames were already a head taller than he was and had spread through where the column had marched. He wondered where all of the other men had gotten to, but had little energy to spend on the thought as he angled to get around the moving edge of the fire while trying to avoid putting his foot in another hole.

The wagon came into sight just beyond the wall of fire. He was going to make it. He could get through the thin offshoot of flame here, and then he would be safely under the wagon. Once he got there, he would see about getting himself one of those grass covered outfits the injuns were wearing.

He stumbled, gut lurching as his feet left the ground. Pain exploded through his shoulders and his feet dangled uselessly below him. He couldn't move his arms. Above him, a giant bird let loose a piercing cry as mighty wings pumped to lift them up into the sky.

"Bart! Bart!" Someone yelled his name and he looked down just in time to see Ryan raise his rifle and fire. A dull pain burned through his skull, making him sick and dizzy. The world started to fade.

*Good shot, Ryan. Thank you. You weren't so useless after all...*

The pillow was soft, but the ache in his arms called to him, pulling him out of slumber. He blinked and looked around, unable to see anything but a white haze.

His chest constricted as he tried to sit up and found could hardly move either arm. He brought up a weak hand and brushed at his face. Slowly the white haze parted.

Feathers. He was in a sea of fine downy feathers. He tried to blow them off his lips and pull them from his nose. The effort was agony on his upper chest and shoulders, but at last he could see blue sky above him.

Probing fingers found the painful gash on his head under his matted hair. *Damn you, Ryan. You couldn't even kill me right.* Dried blood covered his face and had caked into his clothes. Gingerly testing another source of pain, he figured both of his collar bones were broken.

He fought to sit up, but with little use of his arms, it was hard going. When he finally got his feet under him, Bart stood, arms limp at his sides, and swayed, dizzy and weak.

He was in a giant nest, made of twigs the size of his arms. He took a wobbly step and looked over the edge, down the thousand foot cliff, and across the valley.

It was the most beautiful sight he had ever seen—except for the pair of giant eagles flying toward him.

Panic constricted his chest and caused more pain. He tore his eyes from the birds and desperately began looking for an escape. There was no way he could climb the cliffs, even had his arms been uninjured.

He spotted another nest farther down the cliff. Something moved in it. Chicks. Chicks nearly the size of a man.

The scrawny looking beasts batted their heads against each other as they fought over something, stealing it from each other's mouths. Something that was just barely too big to swallow. He took a stumbling step back, recognition setting in, as one of the birds swung the thing around by the long, curly white hair attached to it.

A hissing noise caught Bart's attention. Behind him, a chick tottered up, out of the layer of feathers, its young head lolling on its neck.

Bart panicked, frantically looking around for anything his weakened arms could possibly use as a weapon.

The chick hissed again, and this time clucked, like it was calling him.

Bart risked a look back and frowned. "What the hell?" His eyes had to be tricking him. An arm waved at him from under one of the wings, beckoning him to come closer. The hand stopped and pointed out to the valley, to where the two giant eagles had nearly arrived, and then hurriedly motioned again.

28

The chick was dead. Someone was holding it up, hiding under the bird, using it for camouflage. And they were inviting him to share.

With a quick glance at the approaching giant birds, Bart gratefully hurried over.

He froze when he locked gazes with the Indian holding up the carcass. The long wound across the Indian's face left no doubt as to who it was.

"Well ain't that the ..."

The piercing shriek of a giant bird drowned Bart out as it landed at the edge of the nest.

Bart made a run for the Indian and the dead chick.

The Indian easily caught Bart in the chest with one foot and sent him sprawling. Bart flopped, unable to right himself with his useless arms.

The Indian grinned savagely at Bart and went into a war dance. Walking the chick's body forward, shaking its head up and down, mouth up, the Indian called out with a hoarse cry. A feeding cry.

"Get outta here, runt!"

Georgie managed to dodge the cuff aimed at his ear, but the boot caught him in the seat of the pants and sent him sprawling out through the door and halfway down the flight of stairs. He could barely hear Miss Lacey's protests over the cowboy's guffaws as the door slammed shut.

Georgie lay where he had landed for a moment, elbow hooked around one of the railing uprights for support, and glared at the backdoor of the brothel. He understood that when it was time for the women to work he had to leave, but he didn't appreciate being tossed out.

It was hard enough being ten years old, but being the bastard son of a dead whore and shorter than the local five and six year olds made him the town outcast and the target of constant harassment. If Miss Lacey hadn't insisted on taking him under her wing after his mother had died… Well, any delusions he'd had about life had been beaten out of him long ago.

He picked himself up and stomped down the rest of the rickety wooden steps. When he reached the bottom, he stooped and picked up a rock. He hefted it in his small hand before throwing it as hard as he could at the door.

His aim was true, but, based on the squeals he heard coming from behind the door, the rock went unnoticed.

He ran like hell, just in case.

"Guaranteed to fix what ails you! Uncle Benjamin's Triple 'T' Tonic is Tried, True, and Tasty! It don't come cheap, but then you get what you pay for!"

Lying in the cool dust under the General Store's wooden walkway, where he could enjoy the shade, Georgie chewed a small piece of stolen tobacco and watched the show as someone calling himself "Uncle Benjamin" hawked his wares to a dozen of the local townspeople.

Uncle Benjamin, a short, squat man with an unruly mop of thinning hair, dressed like a dandy, but his foppish blue outfit was sweat stained beyond salvation; salt crystals, nearly as bright as his lacey white cuffs, ringed his underarms.

"My assistant Charles was so satisfied he left his old life behind to help spread the word." Uncle Benjamin waved a thick-fingered hand toward a bald black man dressed in a red outfit just as foppish, and just as worn, as his own.

Charles grinned toothlessly and raised a hand high to the crowd.

"Charles, why don't you tell the fine folk of Little Big Rock just exactly what Uncle Benjamin's Triple 'T' Tonic did for you?" Uncle Benjamin motioned for his assistant to step up onto the plank of wood serving as a stage behind the prairie schooner they'd arrived in.

Georgie Whitcomb found himself grinning back at the black man. That toothless smile was infectious and as full of the joy of life as anything Georgie had ever seen.

"I-I-I know y-y-you good folks will f-f-find this hard to believe," Charles stuttered, but his smile never wavered, "but I was born a slave." He looked around at the people in the crowd. They appropriately feigned surprise and Charles seemed all the more pleased about it. "Yessir! B-b-but what's even harder t' believe is that when…when…" His smile faded and he looked down at the ground. "When I was seven years of age," he looked back up and Georgie was sure he could see tears in Charles' eyes, "I-I-I tol' a lie.

"My punishment, as I'm sure you all noticed right off, was I had my teeth knocked out." Charles opened his lips wide to show his empty gums. "But that weren't all. Oh, no. I-I-I was told that since I wasn't using my voice for truthin', I wouldn't be usin' it 'tall." He opened the front of his red jacket and moved the yellowing lace away from his throat, revealing a mass of scar tissue. "I-I-it wasn't enough that they cut out my tongue. No sir! They done took out my voice box, too!"

Someone in the crowd gasped and Charles and Uncle Benjamin nodded solemnly at them.

"So why is it then, that I-I can stand up here and t-talk to you fine folk?" Charles' smile returned in its full glory. "Because I was fortunate enough to meet Uncle Benjamin and drink his T-t-triple 'T' Tonic! I swear to you, it made my tongue and my voice box grow back! T-t-the only reason I t-t-talk like this, is because I'm still a learning how again!"

Charles' excitement was so contagious that spontaneous applause broke out from the crowd. "You can even see where m-m-my tongue growed back!" He opened his mouth wide and stepped down off the stage into the crowd. Walking around he let them all take turns looking into his grinning, toothless maw.

"What else can it do?" The banker's wife, Mrs. Milton waved her parasol to get Uncle Benjamin's attention.

"Madam, I don't want to say it can do anything, but I can honestly say I've yet to find a limit to what it can do."

"You ain't said what it costs!" Someone yelled. A chorus of agreements echoed the sentiment.

Uncle Benjamin held his arms out wide to calm the crowd. "That's right. I haven't said what it costs." He dropped his voice and everyone had to move closer to hear his next words. Georgie could barely make them out.

"I'm not like other 'snake oil' salesmen. I fully guarantee my product, and I will stay right here, in this town until each and every person who buys Uncle Benjamin's Triple 'T' Tonic comes up to me and tells me they are satisfied. Only then will I move on to the next town. Never heard an offer like that before, have you?"

Murmurs went through the crowd again.

"You still ain't said what it costs!"

Uncle Benjamin stood up straight and tugged at his jacket hem, smoothing it out. "Take a good long look, my friends. Look closely at Charles and myself. Look at our wagon. Is it not apparent to you that we are of modest means?"

Someone grumbled and Uncle Benjamin nodded knowingly at them. "I have not named a price, because the price is different for each of you."

Moans of disbelief came up from the gathered people.

"Please. Hear me out. The clothes upon our backs," he motioned to Charles and himself, "the food in our wagon, yea, even our wagon itself are all payments we have received. We do not ask for money. Sometimes Uncle Benjamin's Triple 'T' Tonic will not work if paid for in mere money. It has to be paid with the most you can afford to give."

"Charlatan!"

"Swindler!"

"Please!" Uncle Benjamin held his hands up again. "Uncle Benjamin's Triple 'T' Tonic is not like anything else you have ever encountered. It is truly a magic potion. I learned how to make the tonic from a powerful medicine man whose life I had saved. He was the last of his kind, and in thanks for my saving him, and so that the wisdom of his people would not be lost forever, he showed me how to make his people's magic. But the magic of the tonic will only work for those who need it the most, and who are willing to sacrifice the most. I promised you I would stay until everyone who purchased Uncle Benjamin's Triple 'T' Tonic was satisfied. If it doesn't do what you need it to, if the magic doesn't work for you, I will give back whatever you paid. It is my guarantee. How much better can it be? Go home and think about it. Come back when you've made up your mind. I will be here."

Art Gray, a local ranch hand Georgie had seen drunk every Saturday night for as long as he could remember, stepped up and held out what looked like a ten dollar bill. Georgie choked on his tobacco. Ten dollars was more than a week's wages for Art.

Uncle Benjamin refused the money. "I meant it. If you buy it with plain old money, it likely won't do what you need it to. You need to figure out what the most, the absolute most you can afford to pay for it is, then, if you really need it to work, it will."

"Ten dollar is all I got! How can I pay more'n what I got?"

"You don't have anything else that's more valuable to you? Nothing in the whole wide world?"

Art looked disgusted. "What kind of salesman are you?"

A tight fist grabbed Georgie by the ankle and dragged him out from under the wooden porch, scraping his knees and elbows on the gravel.

"You little bastard! I done tol' you not to be under there scarin' off my customers!" Mr. Walls, the General Store owner held Georgie's ankle high in the air, causing Georgie to flail wildly. "I'm a whip you but good this time, boy!"

"Please! I didn't mean nothin'! I was just watchin'!"

Mr. Walls ignored Georgie's pleas and grabbed the small roughhewn piece of lumber used to prop open the General Store door. In a deft motion, he pulled down Georgie's trousers, flipped the boy over, and paddled his bare bottom.

"It ain't fair!" Georgie sobbed as Miss Lacey used a pair of tweezers to remove splinters from his buttocks. "I can't walk around, else they kick me and throw things at me. I can't hide, on accounta they say I'm sneakin' round and beat me for it. Hell! They don't even let me go to church!"

"And with a mouth like that, it's no wonder." Miss Lacey gently chastised him. She held him across her lap much the way Mr. Walls had, but her administrations were quite different.

"You don't talk like that, and they don't let you go. How're we supposed to be good God Fearin' Christians when they won't even let us go to church?" Georgie stared at the worn bed, lower lip sticking out, trying to pay attention to what Miss Lacey was saying and not what she was doing.

"We turn the other cheek."

"I ain't never hit no one back, but they keep hittin' me! I only got two cheeks."

"That phrase ain't always meant to be takin' literal."

Georgie glanced around the little room he shared with Miss Lacey. The bed, a nightstand, a small dresser, and the chair Miss Lacey sat in were the extent of the furnishings, their possessions.

His eyes fell upon the blanket in the corner. That was his bed now. At the coming of spring, Miss Lacey had decided he was too old to share the bed with her anymore. He hadn't minded so much. The floor wasn't as comfortable, but it didn't stink like unwashed cowboys and sex like the bed did.

"There we go. I think that's all of them."

"Thank you, Miss Lacey." Georgie stood and pulled up his pants.

"Stay away from Mr. Walls and his store, hm?"

"Do you ...?" Georgie stopped, unable to formulate his question.

"What?"

Georgie looked into the tired face of the only person in town who'd had the decency to care for him after his mother had died. Miss Lacey was no longer young. It wouldn't be too many more years before the cowboys stopped coming to her, then who would take care of him? She wouldn't even be able to take care of herself.

"Do you ever think maybe we should pack up and head out somewhere else?"

A sad smile creased Miss Lacey's face. "Where would we go? What would we do? We have nothing, and we have no way to get anywhere. Besides, what makes you think things would be any different anywhere else?"

"We wouldn't have to tell them you're a whore and I'm a bastard. We could tell them you're my mom, and I'm your kid! Then we could go to church! People would be nice to us..." Georgie's eyes flicked back and forth, searching Miss Lacey's face as his excitement grew. "There's someone here, right now! He's selling tonic! I bet he'd let us travel with him to another town!"

"Ah, Georgie. You know those salesmen ain't selling nothing worthwhile."

"I know. I'm not talking about buyin' anything. Just travlin' with him a ways. I bet if we offered to help—"

"No. Georgie. No. You don't have any idea what you're talking about. Now get outta here. Go on! Get!"

Miss Lacey swatted at his sore behind as she shooed him out the door in spite of his protests.

Sullenly, Georgie walked down the wooden stairs and thought about what he had said wrong. He knew he must have said something wrong, because he'd seen the tears in Miss Lacey's eyes, and she never cried.

"What's this?" Uncle Benjamin eyed the object held out in Georgie's hand, but he didn't reach for it.

"It's my payment. For the tonic. You said we had to pay as much as we can afford, and this is the only thing I own, so it has to be as much as I can afford, right?"

Uncle Benjamin gently reached out and took the small gold locket from Georgie's hand.

Charles walked out from behind the wagon and squatted down to look Georgie in the eyes. "H-h-how old are you, son?"

"Ten years old, sir."

"S-s-sir?" Charles chuckled. "W-w-we got us a b-b-boy who's going places, here, Uncle Benjamin. T-tell me son, why do you want some of Uncle Benjamin's Triple 'T' Tonic?"

"Because you said it can fix anything, sir."

Charles chuckled again. "You don't have to call me 'sir'. You can call me Charles. And what I meant was w-w-what do you want the tonic to do for you?"

Georgie hesitated. "I want it to make things better."

"Better how?" Uncle Benjamin asked. "What can the tonic do that would make things better for you? You seem perfectly healthy to me, son."

Georgie didn't answer. He didn't want to tell them he was a bastard. Then they'd treat him the same way everyone else did. Maybe tonic couldn't cure being a bastard. But Uncle Benjamin had said he'd never found a limit to what it could do, hadn't he?

"That is all I can afford to pay. I'd like to buy some tonic, please."

Charles looked from Georgie, up to Uncle Benjamin. There was no sign of a smile on either man's face.

"I can't take this from you, son." Uncle Benjamin handed the locket back. "I don't know that you haven't just stolen it from your mother, and I'm not interested in causing problems in this town."

"My mother's dead." The words came out before Georgie realized he was going to say them.

Charles' eyes saddened.

"I'm sorry, son. My answer is no." Uncle Benjamin turned back to his wagon.

The saloon was raucous, even for a Saturday night. Georgie wondered if it was because Uncle Benjamin was in town. He'd overheard several people talking about what they thought the tonic could or couldn't do and debating what Uncle Benjamin had meant by paying the most you could afford.

Even now, he occasionally heard Uncle Benjamin's name out of the cacophony of noise escaping the building.

Georgie sat in silence behind the saloon's outhouse and watched the stars as he ran the chain of his mother's locket through his fingers. It was a good night to be out here. Drunken men stumbling out to use the latrine occasionally lost things, especially if they dropped their drawers and things fell out of their pockets, and dark moonless nights made it more likely they wouldn't notice.

Usually it was small stuff. Some loose change, a bullet or two, a plug of chaw. But sometimes it was more.

Once, he'd found five dollars in a wad of bills just outside the outhouse door. That had been a great discovery. The consequences had been a hard lesson though. He'd given the money to Miss Lacey, who had been just as excited as he was, but when she used the money to buy them new clothes, the brothel manager had beat her for holding out on money.

If he ever found money like that again, things would be different.

A pair of voices stood out from the rest of the noise and Georgie made sure he held still and kept quiet.

"…some damned thing. HA! What about you?" The voice was slurring from drink as it grew louder.

"I figured I'd head to the cathouse. I seem to remember having a pretty good time last time I was here."

Georgie's heart nearly stopped. He recognized that voice. He'd heard it the night his mother had been beaten to death.

"Sounds like fun. I might hafta do that myself."

Streams of urine began splattering on the ground next to the outhouse as both men chose to forego entering the little building.

Georgie felt as though he couldn't breathe. He looked down at the locket in his hand, glinting dimly in the starlight. The man who had killed his mother had come back. And he was going back to the whorehouse.

Miss Lacey.

Georgie was on his feet and running. He had to warn Miss Lacey. He couldn't let her get hurt!

"Hey! What the hell was that?" The drunken man called into the darkness behind Georgie.

"A kid!" The other man's voice jarred with footfalls and Georgie looked back, horrified to find he was being chased.

"Stop! You little shit! What were doin' back there? You steal something?"

The man was fast and Georgie cursed his short legs as his pursuer gained on him. He caught Georgie at the foot of the staircase leading up to Miss Lacey's.

Georgie sprawled as the man punched him in the back of the head. Falling into the stairs, Georgie hit his face on a step and white pain flashed behind his eyes.

"Whatcha got in your hand, little thief?" The man grabbed Georgie's wrist and pried the locket from his fist.

"No! It's mine—"

A punch to the cheek cut Georgie's protests off.

"You were stealin'!"

"What's going on out here?" Light spilled over them as Miss Lacey opened up the door.

"This runt was out thievin' tonight!" The man held up the locket for Miss Lacy to see.

In the golden lantern light, Georgie could see the man's features. He'd all but forgotten what the man looked like outside of vague dreams and nightmares. Ruggedly handsome, with clear blue eyes, the man didn't look like someone who would beat a woman to death.

But he had. Georgie had seen it.

When the man had discovered Georgie's mother kept him shut in the closet during 'visiting hours', he had beat Georgie for being in the closet, and then beat his mother. Georgie remembered the way the man had continued to hit his mother long after she had stopped moving.

By the time Georgie had been found the next day, the man had been long gone, and no one thought enough of the death of a whore to try to give chase.

"That's his locket. He didn't steal it." Miss Lacey looked down upon the man pinning Georgie down. "Give it back and get off of him."

The man squinted his blue eyes up the whore in the doorway. "I remember you!" He looked down at Georgie. "You're the little shit from the closet! Didn't I learn you nothin' last time? Now you're a thief?" The man threw another quick punch, hitting Georgie in the eye and bouncing his head off the step again.

"Stop it!" Miss Lacey started down the stairs towards them.

Georgie tried to warn her, but another punch left him reeling.

"And you!" The man stood up, charging up the stairs and meeting Miss Lacey halfway. His fist sunk deep into her stomach and he caught her as she fell. "I can't believe you didn't learn your lesson. A whore, a bad mother, and a thief!" He tossed her over his shoulder as he tromped back up the stairs. "You teach the boy to steal? You tryin' to make sure he goes to hell?"

Georgie struggled to get up, crawling up the steps on his hands and knees as fast as he could. "No! Stop!" Bloody lips made it hard to form the words.

The man turned at the top of the stairs and looked down upon Georgie, shaking his head. "Poor kid." When Georgie reached the top of the stairs, a boot caught him under the chin and sent him all the way back down to the bottom.

It was dark when Georgie awoke. Clouds had rolled in and hidden the stars. The only light crept out from around the edges of the door at the top of the stairs.

His face was swollen. A lump on his head ached and throbbed. His chest hurt horribly. A coughing spasm ended with him spitting up blood.

Miss Lacey.

Georgie scrambled to his feet, ignoring the pain, and ran up the stairs. The door wasn't latched and opened easily under his hand.

Miss Lacey was sprawled across the bed, her shredded clothing strewn around the room, her body bloody.

A gasp escaped from Georgie as he hurried to her, eyes clouding with tears.

When he saw her take a breath, he nearly fainted with relief and tears began flowing in earnest.

Georgie stood outside the front of the saloon and peered in through the wooden slats over the windows. The man who had killed his mother and beaten Miss Lacey sat at a faro table, laughing, drinking, and playing cards as though nothing had happened. And he was twisting the chain of the locket between his fingers.

He still had dried blood on his hands, but no one seemed to notice, or care.

Georgie set his jaw as he decided he was never going to turn the other cheek again, and he set out in search of an unguarded firearm.

"W-w-what the hell you doin', boy?"

The shutter of a storm lantern flipped open and flooded Georgie and the inside of Uncle Benjamin's wagon with light. Charles held the lantern high. He had no sign of the jovial smile Georgie had seen before.

"You trying to steal tonic?"

Georgie looked at the scars on Charles' throat and thought better about lying to the man.

"No. I was looking to see if you had a gun. I just need to borrow it for a few minutes."

Charles' toothless jaw gaped. "B-b-borrow a gun?" The smile returned, spreading wider than Georgie would have thought possible. "What you need to 'borrow' a gun for?" Then the smile quickly faded. "What happened to your face? Someone beat you?"

Georgie swallowed hard. "The man who killed my mother came back tonight. He beat me and … the lady who takes care of me. I aim to stop him before he leaves town again. Do you have a gun I can borrow or not?"

"We do not." Uncle Benjamin stepped up from the darkness behind Charles. "And even if we did, I could not conscionably allow you to 'borrow' it to kill a man."

"The hell with you!" Georgie blurted. "If you would have just taken my payment and given me some tonic, this never would have happened! Everything would have been better. Now I can't even pay you anymore! He stole my locket. He beat up Miss Lacey so bad she won't wake up…" Georgie's words were lost to great racking sobs. His lip split open and began bleeding again.

"I-I-I think maybe the boy is ready for some tonic after all."

Georgie's hands shook as he gently tried to pour tonic from the tiny brown bottle into Miss Lacey's mouth. The liquid that came out was thick like honey, and it piled upon her lips without going in.

"L-l-let me help." Charles reached out and used his thumb to pull down Miss Lacey's swollen lower lip. The syrupy liquid began to flow down into her mouth and across her bloody teeth. When the bottle was empty, Georgie pulled it back. It had held little more than a couple of teaspoons.

"Now what?" Georgie handed the bottle back to Uncle Benjamin.

"Now we wait and see if it works." The thick man smiled gently at the boy.

"It really does work, right? You're not a charlatan?"

Charles smiled his wondrous smile. "I-i-it really does work."

"Sometimes." Uncle Benjamin corrected him. "It really does work only for those who need it the most, and are willing to sacrifice the most."

"I'm sorry I had nothing left to give. Thank you for giving some to Miss Lac—" A coughing fit overcame Georgie. He choked and gasped until he finally vomited blood in the corner of the room.

"T-t-that's not a good sign."

"Pull up your shirt, boy." Uncle Benjamin stepped closer. "How bad did you get beat?"

Georgie lifted his shirt, revealing large purple splotches.

Charles whistled. "Them's broke ribs for sure. Prolly, lot worse under the ribs. I can't believe he been walkin' and talkin'."

Uncle Benjamin reached into his vest pocket and pulled out a second bottle of tonic. "Take this, son. I hope it helps."

---

Georgie strode into the saloon, his head held high, the set of his jaw proud and strong.

Mr. Walls stood up from a table at the sight of the boy and moved to intercept him. Georgie stopped to look at Mr. Walls. Barefooted and raggedly dressed, Georgie met the man's eyes, daring Mr. Walls to do or say anything.

Mr. Walls hesitated.

Georgie's chest swelled with pride at his own courage, and he moved past Mr. Walls to where the man who had beat him sat at the card table.

Confusion crossed Mr. Walls' face as Georgie walked past him. Befuddled looks from others followed as Georgie strode confidently through the saloon, but he ignored them. He walked over to the card table where the man with the blue eyes sat.

"Thief! Give me back my locket."

The man looked Georgie up and down. His brow furrowed, then his eyes narrowed as recognition set in.

"I don't know what you're talking about, boy, but you best learn to respect your elders." The man glanced at the others around him and tried to laugh it off

Georgie pointed to the man's clenched fist. "You've got my mother's locket in that hand. You took it from me. I want it back."

People in the saloon were listening now.

Georgie stepped closer and raised his voice. "You killed my mother four years ago, and now you have the nerve to come back and steal the only thing of her I've got left? Give me back what's mine, thief!"

Anger flashed in the man's blue eyes as he tried to backhand Georgie, but Georgie was too quick and stepped back out of reach.

The man rose slowly, lips snarling. "I told you, boy. Now I'm gonna teach you some manners!"

"Just like you did earlier tonight when you kicked me down the stairs and then beat Miss Lacey and left her for dead—just like you did my mother?"

Murmurs ebbed through the crowd.

The man had his hand on his gun. "You've got a mouth on you kid."

"You draw that gun, mister, and I'll see you dead." Georgie's tone brought the saloon to silence.

The man laughed and looked around to see if anyone else saw how ludicrous the situation was.

"Kid, what the hell makes you think I should be afraid of you?"

Georgie reached out and gently set a little brown bottle on the table. "Does anyone recognize that bottle?" he called aloud without taking his eyes off his foe. "It's Uncle Benjamin's Triple 'T' Tonic! Guaranteed to fix what ails you!"

He met the man's gaze and whispered. "Remember what you did to me earlier? The punches to my face? How do those cuts and bruises look to you now?"

The man stopped and looked closely for the first time. There were no cuts or bruises. Not even a scab or a scrape.

"There's magic in those bottles," Georgie whispered. "And it ain't the card-trick kind." He raised his finger and pointed to the fist holding his mother's locket. "I'm going to tell you one more time. Give me back my locket…Thief."

The man stood still, anger playing across his face. Slowly he held out his hand and opened it.

The locket, exposed for all to see, still had blood on it. Georgie plucked the locket away.

In a flash, the man drew his gun and fired. Georgie no longer stood in front of him. The bullet hit Mr. Walls in the shoulder and spun him around, dropping him to the floor in a sitting position.

The people in the room gasped, some ducking, others frozen.

Georgie, now standing behind the man, reached forward and snatched the gun away. Somehow, in the dim, smoky, lantern lit saloon, he seemed larger than he had been before, almost as big as the man he now held a gun to.

"Have you ever heard of a Spirit Warrior?" Georgie asked quietly. He tapped the gun barrel against the man's ribs. "I hadn't. Not until just a little while ago, when the Wind whispered it into my ear, and told me that's what I was." Georgie let the barrel of the gun slide down the man's side. "A Spirit Warrior chosen by the Spirits themselves to right the wrongs of men."

Standing tall, Georgie moved away from the man and looked around. "Do none of you fine citizens recognize this man?"

No one answered.

"Five years ago, this man murdered my mother in front of me, and none of you cared." Georgie pointed the gun, aiming back and forth across the room. "He just shot Mr. Walls, and I still don't see any of you doing anything about it. Why? It was one thing when this man beat a bastard child and killed his whore mother, but this is quite a different thing, isn't it? Mr. Walls is a fine upstanding man! Mr. Walls only beat on bastard children, too! Not *your* children, not *your* wives!"

Nervous faces glanced back and forth at each other.

"Fortunately for all of you, you didn't allow me to attend church with you, or I would be just like you. And then God only knows what I would do right now." He tossed the gun toward the saloon entrance where it landed at the feet of Charles, Uncle Benjamin, and Miss Lacey. None of them moved to retrieve it.

"If I *was* like you, what would I do?" Georgie looked around accusingly. "Throw rocks at you, maybe? Kick you when you're down?" He glanced at where Mr. Walls still sat on the floor, holding his shoulder, blood leaking between his fingers. "Condemn you for things you got no control over?"

Georgie waited for an answer, but none came. His lips curled in disgust.

"Don't worry. A good woman taught me how to be a good Christian in spite of your best efforts. She taught me to forgive. To turn the other cheek. And God help me, that's what I'm going to do. Again."

Georgie began walking toward the door. Toward Miss Lacey, whose face was now as healthy looking as ever, toward Uncle Benjamin, who looked proud as any father ever had, and toward Charles, who wore a grin as wide and open as the sky.

The man with the blue eyes made a quick motion and a knife flew through the air at Georgie's back.

Impossibly quick, Georgie spun around, his hand flashed out and, plucking the knife from the air, sent the weapon back the way it had come. The knife sunk deep into the man's throat.

In the blink of an eye, Georgie was back in front of the man who towered over him by more than two feet. "I already turned my cheek twice for you. I only got two cheeks. I can't say I'm sorry I couldn't do it again."

Clutching at the knife in his throat, the man slowly sunk to his knees. Georgie turned his back and walked away.

"Wait…" Mr. Walls tried to reach out as Georgie walked past, but his wounded shoulder pained him too much. "Wait…"

Georgie stopped, and for the first time in his life, looked down upon one of the people who had treated him so horribly, and knew their fate was completely in his hands.

"Is he really the man who killed your mother?"

Georgie nodded.

"He admitted as much," Miss Lacey added from the doorway, "while he was beating me." Her eyes flickered as the man fell over, still clutching at his throat and gurgling.

Georgie looked from Mr. Walls to the man who had killed his mother. He turned his back to both of them and faced the three people in the doorway.

Although fully healed, Miss Lacey still had dried blood matted in her hair. Uncle Benjamin and Charles both still had blood on their hands from helping clean Georgie and Miss Lacey up.

"Uncle Benjamin," Georgie raised his voice to make sure everyone could hear. "I'm satisfied with the results of your Triple 'T' Tonic. I feel you have fulfilled your guarantee and promise to me. I give you permission to move on to the next town. When you go, Miss Lacey and I would like to accompany you."

## Colorado

## 1891

D amnation! Look at the size of that sumbitch!"
Gable grimaced, irritated at the sound of Parker's hissed words.

The little man continued whispering without taking his eyes off the buck. "It's big as an elk!"

The mule deer stood on the mountain across the gulch below, nearly three hundred yards away, looking at the two men standing next to their four horses. The buck's rack carried eight points on either side. It didn't move. Not even an ear twitch.

"See 'im?" Parker asked, still looking around the neck of the packhorse he had been unloading.

"I see. Why don't you shoot him?" Gable chuckled to himself as he admired the animal.

"You know my baby ain't got that kind of range." Parker gave the big red-headed man a sideways look. The two men had been arguing over the value of Parker's new .22 pump action rifle for the last two weeks.

This was the first time the men had gone out together, and Gable had quickly regretted his choice of companion. Not only did the little man's incessant talking and complaining grate on him, but they were a week out of where Gable thought they ought to be, and he was irritated at Parker's insistence on coming all the way out here. Tension between the two men had started to come out in the little things—like the usefulness of

Parker's gun.

With Parker's admission that his rifle couldn't make the shot, Gable grunted in satisfaction and eased his own Hawken .50 caliber out of his saddle holster, laying it across the back of his horse. Other than the distance, he couldn't ask for a better shot.

The buck still stared at them across the valley, unmoving and perfectly silhouetted in the middle of a melting patch of snow.

Gable whispered to his horse, letting it know he was about to fire. A good trail horse, it held still as he aimed across its saddle and pulled the set trigger, readying the rifle for a shot. He exhaled and pulled the second trigger. The muzzleloader cracked the silence of the piney forest and a plume of blue smoke drifted from where the hammer had dropped. One of the pack horses startled, but it was tethered to Gable's horse and unable to pull away from the better trained animal.

"Hooeey! You dropped him like a rock! That was a hell of a shot." Parker slapped his hat on his leg in excitement. "We ain't eating no sonofabitch stew tonight!" He grinned wide, his greasy black hair plastered to his head.

Gable grinned wryly, satisfied he had shown up the little man's rifle. His right eye watered from the powder smoke as he squinted at the empty snowy patch. "I don't see him."

"He din't go nowheres. He fell like a sack of taters."

Gable kept his eyes on the spot while he poured more gunpowder down the barrel of his rifle. He thought he had made a good shot, but it bothered him he couldn't see the carcass in the snow. He used the ramrod to push the patch and ball down into the Hawken, but still nothing moved. A good sign he had made a clean kill.

"Here," he handed the muzzleloader to Parker once he was done placing a new firing cap under the hammer. "Let me take your Winchester in case I didn't get him clean."

"What, that Colt on yer hip ain't good enough? Oh, I see. You wanna hold my girl for a while." Parker winked and pulled his new Winchester rifle out of its holster. "You treat her right, and don't forget she goes home with me at night." He traded rifles with Gable. "She ain't no one-shot whore. I paid more'n twenty dollar for her."

"Walk me in." Gable ignored the jibe and started towards the kill. Parker's rifle felt light and fragile in his oversized hands. He lumbered down the rocky slope into the scrub oak marking the wash between the mountains. Dried leaves and branches crackled and snapped with his passing as he scraped through.

"You a noisy bastard, ain't cha?" He heard Parker laughing at him. "Good thing they ain't no injuns 'round her no more, or they'd have your scalp for sure!"

Gable wondered if Indians wouldn't shoot the idiot yelling first. He came out of the thicket on the far slope and turned to look back. Parker had begun repacking the horses. Gable approved of the man's actions for a change. It would be easier to bring the horses to the kill than it would be to drag the carcass all the way back. He whistled to get Parker's attention.

Parker looked up at Gable, then took his hat off and held it straight up in the air with his skinny arm.

Gable turned and kept walking up the mountain, working his way around a large boulder pile and then backtracking when he was blocked by a dense growth of trees. Back around the boulder pile, he stopped and turned for directions again.

Parker held his hat out to the right and Gable moved that way until he found the patch of snow.

Gable walked a circle around the snow patch. There were no tracks, no blood. He walked the snow patch again, this time in a wider circle. Nothing. There was no sign of the buck.

He whistled again. Parker turned to look at him and Gable spread his arms wide.

"It's right there, idjit!" Parker hollered across the draw. He took off his hat again, waving it in a circle to tell Gable he was already there. Gable walked one more circle around the snow patch and stopped with his arms spread wide again.

Parker flopped his arms down at his sides with over-exaggerated exasperation and waved his hat again. "Just look for the damn tracks already!"

Gable dropped his arms and began walking back to camp, ignoring Parker's waving hat.

"You don't like where he fell? We need to find another

one to shoot?" Parker paced, irritated, as Gable approached.

"There's nothing there," Gable answered. "You walk me into the right patch of snow?"

They both looked back at the mountain. There was only one patch of snow.

Parker shook his head in disgust. "You take the horses and meet me up there."

Gable shrugged and passed off the repeating rifle as the skinny man went by him in a huff. He tried hard to keep his own annoyance off his face. Not for the first time, Gable wondered why he had paired off with Parker.

He watched Parker walk up the mountain and around the patch of snow. Parker stepped out into the snow. His boots sunk readily into the melting snow. Walking to the center of the white patch, he turned around in a circle, looking. He took of his hat, scratched his head angrily, and cursed at the sky. "I know you was right here, you sumbitch!"

His reedy voice carried back and Gable smirked at his frustration. Tying all four horses together, he led them up the slope, arriving as Parker finished his fifth circle looking for tracks.

"I told you there wasn't anything here."

"It's the only snow on the whole goddamn mountain! I saw it. You shot it. It was here." Parker held his arms wide, hat still in his hand.

"Well there's nothing here now, and I don't want to make camp on the cold side of the mountain. You want to move on, or go back where we were?"

Gable did his best to ignore Parker as the man repeatedly spun the cylinder on his revolver and stared out at the purple twilight. The setting sun left behind the false dusk of the Rocky Mountains, holding the night at bay a little longer. They had moved on over the next ridge before making camp, but they had never seen any sign of the buck.

"I still cain't believe that dead deer up and walked away," Parker muttered as he spun the cylinder again.

Gable shook his head in disgust. He was irritated with the clicking sound of Parker playing with the pistol. "You're going to keep worrying at that 'til it bleeds. I missed the shot."

"Then why ain't there no tracks?"

"We went to the wrong place."

"The Hell we didn't!"

Gable spat some loose coffee grounds off the tip of his tongue at the campfire. "Are you going to turn this into some kind of a ghost story? Tell everyone to stay out of these mountains on account of there's a big buck you can't kill lives up here?"

Parker looked sharply up at the big man. "Old Snorter!"

"What?"

"Five years ago, when I come through Cañon City the first time, there was an ol' timer livin' in the bottom of a bottle at the saloon. He tol' story about a big ol' buck called Old Snorter. Said there's a Spanish gold mine up in the mountains, a cursed one o'course, and it was protected by Old Snorter."

Gable grunted into his coffee tin as he took the last swallow.

"The old man said it couldn't be kilt. Said he shot it four, mebbe five, times, and it would just vanish! Said it was protecting the mine, would show up whenever they got close to it; try to keep 'em away from it." Parker's eyes were wide as he repeated the story. "He said he was the only one of a party of six what made it out alive after finding the cursed mine!"

"Who ever heard of a mule deer protecting anything, let alone a mine?" Gable shook the coffee dregs out of the bottom of his cup, took a bite off his chaw plug, and leaned back on his bedroll.

"Old man said it was some kinda injun magic, a spirit totem, to keep people away. Kept talking 'bout how he wished to God they'd let that buck chase 'em off."

Gable spit into the fire, and listened to the sizzle, trying to ignore Parker's nonsense.

"Wouldn't that be somethin'?" Parker persisted. "If'n we found ourselves an old Spanish gold mine up here? That old man wouldn't talk 'bout no mine though. Alls he kept sayin' was it's cursed."

"You get yourself all spooked, and you're going to have a long night, Parker."

Parker sat up restlessly, holstered his revolver, and poked at the fire. "Would beat the hell out of sellin' hides, for sure. Don't hardly pay nothin' no more. Ain't hardly nothin' up here no more, neither."

A loud cough echoed from somewhere in the forest behind Parker as he finished the words.

Gable chuckled. "There's still something up here."

Parker turned to look into the darkening forest. "Somethin' big, sounds like. Reckon we got a grizzly coming to see what's what?" The wiry man slid out his repeating rifle without taking his eyes off the woods.

"Doubt it. Damn few grizzlies left in Colorado."

Two of the horses snorted nervously. Gable quietly reached out and checked to make sure his Hawken was next to him.

A figure moved silently through the dark trees of the pine forest, a man, barely visible in the night. The man stopped and looked around, as if noticing the campfire for the first time. He snuck closer, staying just out of the firelight. He was a white man, wearing buckskin beaded with intricate patterns by the skilled hand of a squaw. He brought a stubby finger up to his bearded lips, warning Parker and Gable to keep quiet. Then he looked quickly over his shoulder and vanished back into the trees.

Gable slowly pulled back the hammer of his rifle with a quiet click and slunk away from the firelight, towards the nearest tree. He glanced at the horses to see which way their ears were pointed, and focused his attention the same way.

One of the horses snorted and pawed at the ground, and all four began nervously pulling against their tethers.

Parker followed Gable's example and moved away from the firelight, in the opposite direction.

The forest had gone still. The last of the sky darkened and night settled in fully as they waited silently, hearing only the small crackling sounds of the fire. The horses stamped their feet nervously a few times. A long time passed before Parker whispered at Gable.

"I don't see nothin'. You?"

"Cover me," Gable told him, knowing Parker's repeating rifle would protect him better than he could do with his one-shot muzzleloader.

Moving quietly now, unlike tramping through the brush after the deer earlier, Gable circled the campfire, keeping to the shadows and making his way to where the buckskin-clad man had moved through the trees.

The forest was dark, too dark to find any sign of the unknown man's passing, but Gable slinked through the woods like a shadow, first in the direction the man had looked over his shoulder, and then back, following where the man had gone. After finding nothing, he returned to where Parker waited, carefully staying out of the light of the campfire.

"I can't find anything," he told Parker as he settled next to him.

After a long pause staring into the darkness, Parker answered. "I didn't know you was capable of walkin' soft."

"Lot you don't know about me. Reckon we should have killed the fire." Gable worked his way over and kicked dirt over the small flame, smothering it and dropping their world into complete darkness.

"Lot you don't know 'bout me, neither," Parker mumbled back.

A heavy snort, similar to the horses but eerily different, sounded through the forest. Parker turned towards the sound and whispered back to Gable. "Elk?" he asked.

Gable shook his head, not caring Parker couldn't see him, and kept his eyes on the forest, waiting for his night sight to return.

He tensed as he spotted the silhouette of the enormous mule deer staring back at them, its eyes glowing faintly in the starlight. The buck shook his head, threatening them with his antlers. He snorted again, a deep intimidating warning.

Parker fired. The small caliber of his rifle popping three times into the night as Parker worked the pump as fast as he could. The buck vanished.

"Where'd he go?" Parker hissed as he squinted into the darkness, trying to see again. "Goddam it! I know I hit him!"

Gable shook his head, lips pursed as agitation crept over him. Parker shouldn't have been shooting, giving away their position, but even more so, he agreed that Parker had hit the buck. And it had vanished right in front of their eyes.

A strange keening sound reached their ears and Parker stopped his complaining.

"You hear that?" Parker asked hoarsely. "I've heard that sound afore. That's a man. Dying. In a bad bad way." Parker swallowed hard. The little man was visibly shaken

Gable didn't answer. He recognized the sound, too. He didn't know where Parker had heard it, but he had seen the Apache torture a man to death when he was a boy—and it had sounded like that.

A light flickered through the trees in the direction of the horrible sound, and voices followed it.

"I'm mighty glad you put out that fire." Parker's whispered voice, harsh and dry, trembled with fear. "That sounds like injuns."

"They heard the shots. They know where we are." Gable answered. "It's too goddam dark to try to get out of here." He started fumbling in the dark, finding his reloading kit for his Hawken and the spare cartridges for his Colt. "We might have to make a stand for it. How many shots you got left?"

"She holds fifteen, and I only shot three? So's... I got a lot."

"We need to time it so that you and I are never re-loading at the same time. Keep count on your shots, let me know when you only got two left, so I can cover while you reload."

Parker was silent for a moment. "I ain't so good with countin'."

"With your sidearm, you've still got eighteen. Let me know when you switch guns, so I can help you count. Get yourself ready to reload fast."

The light in the trees continued to move closer, but the voices were indistinct as ever. Angry mumbles and unintelligible words floated through the night. Men's voices. The rustles, rattles, and clanks of their movements told Gable there were many of them, and they weren't Indians.

The agonizing wail that had been constant for the last few

minutes cut short with a gurgle. Harsh laughter broke out among the distant voices. The light grew brighter as it approached.

"Get ready," Gable hissed.

Parker swallowed audibly.

Dusky fog lit up in moving beams as the light bobbed through the trees. Shadows of men moved ahead of the light, playing through the beams like ghosts.

"There!" Parker hissed under his breath and pointed his rifle as the first outline came out of the trees—and vanished.

The light went out. The voices stopped.

Gable flinched with his finger on the trigger, nearly firing his weapon. Parker sucked air through his teeth in alarm. One of the horses snorted nervously behind them.

All movement in the forest was gone. The two men sat silent and motionless for a long time, straining their eyes and ears for the men they knew to be in the woods around them, not daring to move or make a sound for fear of giving away their positions.

<hr>

Cold came with the first light of dawn. Gable finally made out the shadowy shape of Parker, asleep with his face pressed against the bark of a tree. He turned his weary eyes back to the place he'd been staring at all night, where they had last seen the light and the moving figures.

His body was stiff, sore, and cold. The night was a daze in his memory, filled with worry he may not be able to pull the trigger with the finger that had remained frozen in position all night. Still, nothing moved as the forest lightened.

Eventually the birds came to life, flitting in the trees and brush, scratching at the leaves and undergrowth for food. The horses nickered at the coming sun. When two squirrels chased each other through the trees he was watching, Gable finally decided the danger was past.

Parker jerked awake, pointing his rifle around nervously. He spotted Gable and relief melted across his face. He tossed a grin at the big man. "Guess they couldn't find us."

"They didn't look for us."

"How long was I out?"

Gable shrugged. "It was a long night."

Parker rolled off the tree and moaned with stiffness. He looked up towards the brightening sky. "Thank ye, Jesus, for not lettin' those injuns get us."

"It wasn't Indians," Gable began working the kinks out of his body too. "Indians don't wander around the night with lights."

"Then who was it?"

"Damned if I know."

"Lookit this!" Parker waved Gable over. "Lookit up there."

The smaller man pointed up the mountain to a cave entrance, half hidden in the shadows of overhanging rocks. The entrance was squared off and looked to be the work of human hands.

"Maybe we really did find Old Snorter and the Spanish gold mine!" Parker was already pulling at his horse's reigns, trying to lead the way up the slope.

Gable watched him for a moment. "Seems to me you said that it was a *cursed* Spanish gold mine."

"Thought you didn't go in for ghost stories?" Parker grinned over his shoulder as he walked on.

"That was before last night," Gable muttered to himself. He had searched diligently throughout the morning and found no signs of men or of a giant buck he knew had been shot.

He shook his head in resignation and followed Parker upslope, weaving around small piñon trees and buck brush. About halfway up the slope, Gable stopped and looked back. There seemed to be a swath where the growth was different somehow. Almost like a path had been cleared at one time.

Then the white spot caught his eye. A different kind of white than snow, bleached bones always stood out bright against rocks and shrubs. Gable stepped closer to see. Scattered ribs and vertebrae could be hard to tell from for sure, but the broken skull was human.

The day grew hot and still, the air heavy around him. He wiped the sweat from his face with his sleeves and stared at the skull. Bones didn't lie on top of the ground like this for very long until they scatter and break apart.

"Parker!" Gable called, but Parker had reached the cave entrance and paid him no attention. He tried to call again, but his throat had gone dry in the heat and he choked on the sound.

Digging water out of his pack, Gable gulped it quickly, splashing some on his face as he did so. The day had become unbelievably hot.

He leaned on the pack horse and looked around at the trees lining what he thought might be an old trail. So many of them were dead, they looked like piles of bones, stacked to get them out of the way. He took another drink before putting the water away. He should go see if they really were piles of bones. They looked like bones.

Then he spotted the old pile of leather at the foot of a tree, downhill from the skull. He tied off the horses to a spindly dead branch that reminded him of giant finger bones, and made his way down to see.

The leather, clothing and a pouch, was hard and stiff, caked into one lump from being in the rain and the sun. He flipped the pile over revealing the beaded pattern sewn into it. Some of the beads fell off and bounced down the rocky slope. It was ruined, but recognizable as the same clothing he had seen on the man in the woods the night before. The flap on the pouch cracked and broke as he opened it. Inside was what he would expect to find in any trapper's kit. Reloading patches, balls, and powder horn, some dried up and moldy chaw and jerky, and a few other things, including a ruined newspaper dated 1886.

He looked back at the skull. If the clothes and bag had belonged to the dead man, then the dead man was a white man, and he had been here around five years. And Gable had seen his ghost.

Five years... The time period stuck in Gable's mind for a moment, then he remembered Parker's story about Old

Snorter. Parker had heard it five years ago.

He looked back at the skull. Was this one of the men from Parker's story? One of the men who didn't come back? Had Parker really brought him to an old Spanish gold mine? If so, was it really cursed?

The more he looked up and down the old trail, the more he felt the trees looked like they were made out of bones.

"Woooohooo!" Parker's voice came down the mountain at him. "Lookit this, boy! Goddamned beautiful! Lookit it!"

Gable looked up and spotted Parker doing a slow jig holding up a rock.

"We are goddamned rich!"

Parker moved around the mine entrance like an ant on its hill. The little man's energy was boundless as he scoured through pebbles and rocks, broken remnants dropped by the miners. Some he tossed down the hill, others he sorted into piles. He shoved a few into his pockets, muttering and giggling to himself the whole time. He seemed to have forgotten Gable was even there.

Gable sat quietly, watching, and thinking. He had tried to talk to Parker about the bones on the sides of the trail, but Parker would hear nothing of it. "Just old sticks," Parker had said when Gable had pressed the issue. And the more Gable looked at them, the more he thought maybe Parker was right, but they sure looked like bones.

He had tried to talk about the clothing and the ghost, but Parker had been irritated at being pulled away from the gold by that time, and had ignored that, too.

Perhaps it was the way the trees here felt like giant skeletons watching over him, but while watching Parker, Gable had been grabbed by another notion, and he couldn't let it go.

Parker had damned near walked them straight into this mine, almost as though he knew it was here. He had set Gable up with a story about a mine, just the night before they found it. He had even given explanation, as victims of the curse, for any skeletons they found.

60

Which, perhaps Parker had known they would.

"We gotta go in!" Parker suddenly stood up and looked around for Gable. "If they left all this gold layin' around out here in the open, imagine what's in there! It must be just fallin' off the walls!"

Parker scurried over to one of the horses and started rummaging in the packs. He came out with a small storm lantern Gable hadn't known was in there. Had Parker known he would need one?

"You comin'?" Parker lit the candle and closed the little metal door on the lamp.

Gable nodded and stood up to follow.

If Parker had killed that man five years ago, and if he intended to kill Gable too, it wouldn't likely be here and now. There must have been some reason for Parker to bring him here. Unless he got greedy for Parker's gold, Gable figured Parker would be wanting to use him to help pack gold out of here, before killing him. Maybe he wanted to find a good place to stash it close to a town, where he could get it himself easy, then he would try to kill Gable.

Following the smaller man into the mine's entrance, Gable kept his distance and tried to stay alert to anything Parker might be up to.

The walls of the mine were roughhewn, work done by the hands of men. The darkness ate up all of the light within ten feet of the mine's mouth. They stopped to let their eyes adjust to the dim candlelight from the small lamp.

The sound of their breathing was heavy in Gable's ears when he heard the clang of metal on rock.

"You hear that?" Parker's whisper was so quiet it was nearly just mouthed.

Gable didn't answer. Could it be Parker had an accomplice? Or maybe someone he thought he had killed, but hadn't, was back to claim the gold for themselves.

"I should go get my rifle." Parker whispered again. "Might be bear, or mountain lion, livin' in here."

Gable bristled at the thought. Then the sound came again, and he was able to pinpoint it. "Or it could be a rat." He pointed further into the cave where a faint gleam could be seen, something reflecting the light back at them. The dark shape of a rodent scampered away from it and into the darkness.

"What's that?" Parker leaned closer without walking forward.

Gable moved nearer to see the silvery thing. "Spanish armor," he told Parker when he got close enough to make it out. Everything about Parker's 'legend' seemed true

He scratched his ear and looked from the breastplate to Parker as he pondered that. Maybe Parker was setting him up for something, but what about the men in the forest, and the vanishing buck? Parker couldn't have done those. Could he? Was there someone else here? Did Parker have an accomplice of some sort? Why the hell would Parker go through all of this trouble?

The dull metallic clank echoed through the mine again, louder this time, and from deeper below. It was not the rat on the armor.

"Knackers?" Parker asked from beside him.

Gable jumped. He hadn't noticed Parker moving closer with the light. The sound had distracted him. He had heard it before; in the night, when the men were walking through the forest. It had been echoed many times, as if all the men were making that sound.

"No. I don't think it's Tommyknockers." He bent down and lightly tapped a fingernail against the breastplate. It sounded with the same flat clunk that came from below.

He thought of the skull outside and the man he had seen in the woods. Had the man's ghost been trying to warn them? Telling them not to disturb the spirits here?

The hair stood up on the back of Gable's neck. This wasn't Parker's doing.

"We have to get out of here," he told Parker. "I think that old man was right. I think this mine is cursed."

Parker wasn't paying attention. He had set the lantern down and was busy examining a rock twice the size of his fist.

"Parker. We have to get out of here."

The clanking sounds increased. There was so much clatter, Gable imagined a legion of Spanish soldiers coming together, getting ready to come marching out. Marching out into the woods by lamplight. That's what they had seen the night before.

"Parker?" Gable put his hand on the man's shoulder.

Parker flinched away from the touch and hissed. "It's mine! Go find your own!"

"We have to get out of here. Now!"

The sounds came closer, growing louder, up out of the hell in the depths of the cave. Parker had no ear for them as he glared at Gable.

"I'm warnin' you! I'm willin' to share the find, but you ain't takin' what's mine! This's gotta be the biggest goddamned nugget anyone ever found!" He clutched the rock close to his chest.

"It's the curse! It's messing with your head. That's nothing but a rock." Gable pointed down into the depths. "They're coming. We have to go."

"Mess with your own head! I don't hear nothin'!"

The sounds grew louder and Gable expected to see the glint of light off metal down in the darkness any second.

"The hell with you." Gable turned and ran back for the glaring light at the tunnel entrance.

"The hell with me? The hell with you!" Parker chased after Gable. "You touch one of those rifles, and I'll kill you first! I'll shoot you in the back if'n I have to!"

He tried to shoulder Gable aside as he passed him. He dropped his rock and it hit another rock, breaking in two. Parker dived for one of the halves and then scrambled to get the other one, glaring at Gable the whole time.

"Parker. Look at the rock. Gold don't break like that. This place is messing with you."

"Just like you and the damned bones, I suppose! You're messin' with me!"

The sounds of voices mixed with the noises coming up from the mine now. Anxious voices. They were hurrying. They were coming for them.

"I'm leaving," Gable told him. "You can keep your 'gold'. I don't want any of it. This place is cursed and I'm getting the hell out of here." He turned and ran out into the sunlight.

Gable stumbled to a stop. The trees had become giant skeletal rib cages and arms, towering over him, reaching for him. He took a step back, out of their reach, back towards the mine and the approaching men.

The horses screamed and pulled at their tethers, snapping the brittle finger bones they had been tied to.

"Damn you, Gable!" Parker yelled and Gable turned to see him running out of the mine as fast as he could with his pistol drawn. He wasn't fast enough.

Soldiers poured out of the darkness, silver armor glinting in the sunlight. Musket fire rang out and Gable felt the bullet rush past his head. He drew his Colt and fired, but the soldiers never slowed. He turned and ran for the horses with Parker chasing after him yelling. More musket fire went by. He felt something hot hit the back of his shoulder and the revolver flew out of his hand. The horse in front of him screamed as a wound opened up in its flank. He grabbed the closest rifle, Parker's repeater, and stumbled backwards, trying to take aim as the soldiers overtook Parker.

He fired as two of them caught up with the little man, their swords flashing as they hacked at him. In an instant, Parker was down, covered with Spanish soldiers who kicked and slashed at him. Gable pumped the rifle and shot again, and again, but there were too many soldiers, he couldn't keep them off Parker.

The horrible keening noise they had heard in the woods the night before started up again, and this time, Gable knew it came from Parker's throat.

Gable fired the rifle blindly into the crowd of armor, pumping it over and over. Soldiers went down, but more kept coming. Gable pumped the action until there were no more shells to be fired. And the soldiers laughed.

They laughed at him as the burning pain in his shoulder finally brought him to his knees, and they closed in slowly around him. One took the reins of Gable's horse, claiming it for his own, laughing as he went through the contents of the saddle bags. Then the soldier leveled a harquebus at him and fired. The old rifle threw off a giant smoke cloud and the impact sent Gable rolling backwards down the hill.

He tried to sit up, but couldn't. He put a hand to his chest, and it came away crimson. Breathing was hard. He looked up into the blue sky and felt the hot sun burning his face. The horrible sound of Parker dying had stopped. He felt a sense of relief that the man wasn't suffering anymore. A movement caught his eye, and he turned his head to look.

The buck stood there, at the edge of the trees, silhouetted by one of the bone piles. It snorted at him and shook its head, flicked its tail, and walked away. Gable thought he could see the shadow of the man who had shushed them following the buck out of sight.

He felt a tear trickling down his cheek. Old Snorter hadn't been protecting the mine after all, he had been trying to warn them. He had been a warning.

"I tol' you, you goddamned ijut!" Parker stumbled down the hill and stood over him, shaking like a leaf. He threw the Hawken rifle on the ground beside Gable. Blood ran from where he had been shot in the arm and the leg. "I tol' you if you touched one of those guns, I'd kill ya!"

<hr>

"What's with the guy and the rock?" The dusty rider asked after he finished his second drink.

The barkeep looked up from behind the bar and glanced at the small man sitting alone in the corner with the fist sized rock on the table in front of him. The man muttered and mumbled to himself while occasionally turning the rock to look at it differently.

"He don't hurt nothin'."

"I didn't reckon he did. I was just curious why he sits there starin' at that rock."

The barkeep lowered his voice. "He thinks it's a chunk of gold."

The rider raised an eyebrow and looked back at the rock on the table.

"He says it's cursed," the barkeep continued, "and that's why we can't see it's actually gold. He sits there and stares at it all day. He'll tell you a good story if you go ask him about Old

Snorter."

The rider laughed. "I got nothin' better to do. I think I'll do that. What's his name?"

"Parker."

The rider placed some money on the bar. "Set me up a drink to take him to pay for the story. I can't figure his cursed gold buys much around her."

Setting a bottle on the bar, the bartender whispered, "If you get him talking, see if you can find out where he got the rock."

"If it's 'cursed' gold, what's it matter?"

The barkeep reached low behind the bar and brought something up. He dropped a few pebbles onto the bar.

The rider leaned in to look close at the tiny golden nuggets.

"Because it ain't all cursed."

by

Sam Knight *and* Rhye Manhattan

# Colorado

# 1878

Who in da hell needs a shtoopid moshito masquine?" The drunken bartender's breath blanketed over Jasper, stealing the air around him and making him gasp.

Jasper backed up two steps. The wood plank floor creaked under him.

"Sir, I assure you, your patrons will notice the difference. They will come to your establishment just to enjoy a few hours of pest free—"

The bartender dismissed Jasper with a loud belch.

Grimacing, Jasper tried once more. "I can leave it at no cost to you. A trial service, if you will…"

"Buy a drink, or get da hell out of my bar!" The bartender glared and spat at the spittoon, missing widely and leaving a shiny new stain among the old dark ones on the floor.

Jasper sighed and politely tipped his gray felt derby hat to the obstinate proprietor. The reaction was not entirely unusual, although the rancid breath was.

Most people just weren't concerned with mosquitos, let alone vampires, out here in the West, and Jasper was finding it difficult to set up a harvesting route between the East and West Coasts. Not for the first time, he wondered if it was wasted effort. All for a good cause or no, there comes a point of diminishing returns.

Jasper stepped across the threshold of the bar and back out into the bright sun of the early afternoon. Squinting into the glare and looking at the dusty prairie beyond the ramshackle town, he considered how far he could get before dark and decided to push on.

He was halfway to his wagon when someone called out behind him.

"Hey, Mister!"

Jasper turned. A gangly boy jogged after him, holding a hand up to shield his eyes. The boy was barefoot, wearing ragged pants and shirt. Dust puffed up from under each footfall, adding to the coating making him a uniform shade of light brown. A grimy red bandana tied around his neck was the only splotch of color on the sandy youth.

"Can I get a ride with you? I can pay." He didn't look well. He was pale and out of breath and, now that he was closer, Jasper could tell the lankiness was partially caused by emaciation. "The stage don't run through here no more, and I can't afford a horse."

The situation was not uncommon. Small settlements across the country had dried up and died with the advent of the new trade routes established by the steam engine railways and the dirigible airways.

"I don't much care where you're headed," the boy pleaded. "I'm trying to work my way somewheres I can catch an airship so's I can get to my grandpa's. Please, Mister. My folks are dead and I got nothin' else out here."

"What happened to your folks?"

The boy's eyes flickered down, but he kept his hand up to shade them. "Indians."

Although unlikely, it was plausible. When the proclamation that all men were truly equal had rung out across the country after the Civil War, some of the Indians had set out to reclaim their land. First by asking, then by taking.

The boy's demeanor told Jasper he was lying.

Jasper looked him over. The ragged clothes, too small for the boy's growing frame, were commonplace out here, as was being skinny enough to see backbone and the haunted look in his eyes. But the pale skin and...

68

"Take the kerchief off your neck."

The boy's eyes widened. "Pardon?"

"You heard me, son. Take the kerchief off from around your neck."

"No, sir." The boy, although shaken, stood firm.

"Someone try to string you up? You runnin' from the law?"

"No, sir!" The sound of wounded pride convinced Jasper that wasn't the case, but concerned him even more. He was pretty sure he knew why the boy wore the garment about his neck.

"How long ago were your parents killed?" He watched the boy's eyes closely.

"Six days."

Jasper cursed. "Let me see the bite."

The boy swallowed hard. "Pardon?"

"Don't play games with me anymore. I can help you, but I need to know everything. Get in the back of the wagon and take off the kerchief so I can see the bite." Jasper pointed to his canvas covered wagon and waited for the boy to make up his mind.

"You can't help me," the boy whispered. "You're gonna stake me in there where no one sees you do it."

"No. I really can help you, but you have to trust me."

They stood and looked at each other, the boy's hand shaking as he blocked the sun from his eyes.

"How did you know?" The boy's lips were tight, pulling his mouth small.

"Vampires killed my family, too. Everyone except my mom. I took care of her for seven days after they bit her. I saw her change. I know what happens. You have another day, at most." Jasper met the boys gaze and held it. "The longer you wait, the less chance I have of helping you."

The boy's shoulders slumped. He nodded as he headed for the wagon.

"Did anyone else get bit and left alive?"

The boy shook his head as he climbed up into the back of the covered wagon. "They killed everyone. Ma, Pa, my little sisters ..."

"How many of them were there?" Jasper asked as he climbed in behind the boy.

"Four, I think. I only saw three, two men and a woman, but I heard them talking to someone else outside."

"That would likely be their bloodscout."

"What's that?"

"Vampires can't stand direct sunlight, so they often have a human who works for them. Scouts out food sources, transportation, places to stay, things like that. You probably heard the bloodscout collecting payment for turning your family into food. You meet anyone lately you think might have sold your family out?"

The boy, who had removed the bandana from around his neck while listening, went slack-jawed at the thought.

Jasper needed little more than a glimpse of the bite to know he had been right. Unlike the red of a normal infection, the surrounding area had begun to turn a pale blue. He pretended to examine the two swollen puncture wounds as he slipped a syringe out of his shoulder bag.

Taking advantage of the boy's momentary distraction, Jasper jammed the needle into the boy's leg and pushed the brass plunger, injecting the boy before he could react.

The boy yelped and jerked back, nearly falling out the back of the wagon.

Jasper held up the shiny instrument for the boy to see before he began carefully cleaning it for storage. "I injected you with anti-venom. If we got it to you in time, you should start feeling better by tomorrow. You're gonna feel like hell tonight though."

The boy's eyes flicked nervously from the syringe to Jasper's face. "What if we didn't get to me in time?"

"You'll be a vampire in two days."

<hr>

The wagon hit a bump in the road, lifting the boy's sleeping form up into the air and dropping him back down soundly onto the wagon's wooden bed. A moan escaped as he woke and fought to sit up.

"Water's in the skin hanging on the right side," Jasper called back over his shoulder.

The boy looked around and spotted the waterskin swaying from a peg on the side of the wagon. He lifted it off and took a long drink of the warm water.

"You feeling any better, Adam?"

The boy wiped a drip off his chin. "How'd you know my name?"

Jasper laughed. "Glad to see you finally pulled through. You must've been closer to turning than I thought. The anti-venom was hard on you."

Adam re-hung the waterskin and crawled to the front of the wagon. He looked around as he climbed out onto the bench with Jasper and agitation crawled across his face.

"You brought me back home to Kansas? Mister, I told you I needed an airship to get to my grandpa's!" Adam tossed his head back and looked up at the heavens in despair. "It took me a week to get to Colorado ..." he groaned.

"You don't remember anything we've talked about the last few days do you?"

"The last thing I remember is you stabbing me in the leg!"

Jasper nodded. "You want me to pretend like we just met all over again? How do you do? My name's Jasper Tidball. I noticed you've been bitten by a vampire—let me help you with that."

Adam gave Jasper a sour look. "How's about you stop the wagon so's I can take a leak while I think about it?"

Jasper pulled the reins and the horses slowed, nickering at the interruption.

Adam clumsily climbed down, using the buckboard to steady himself.

"You're still kind of shaky," Jasper noted as Adam stepped into the shade of the covered wagon. "We should stop for the night and get you rested up before tomorrow."

"What're you talking about?"

"You told me you wanted to be a vampire hunter."

"So the mosquito machines are really just a cover for you to hunt vampires?" Adam poked at the campfire with a stick. The night was just beginning to cool.

"Not entirely." Jasper helped himself to the last of the beans. "They do eliminate mosquitos, but their real purpose is to collect mosquitos and use them to make anti-venom. In places where I find communities fighting vampires, I set one up and show them how to use it. In other places, someone comes through every few months to collect the anti-venom made by the machine."

"How'd you figure to make a vampire cure out of mosquitos?"

"The hard way." Jasper spooned beans into his mouth and talked around them. "I was trying to follow my mother when I ran into a group of vampire hunters outside of New Orleans. We chased a vampire out into the swamps. I was cornered and bit before I could stake him. One of the other hunters staked him from behind as he fed on me. When they saw I had been bit, they tried to stake me, too."

Jasper lifted his shirt to show a ragged scar across his ribcage.

"I barely got away alive. I was in no shape to travel, though, and I couldn't go back into town. They'd have killed me for sure, and I didn't have the guts to let them. I waited to die in that god-forsaken swamp, knowing that if I didn't die out there, I would turn into a vampire, just as I had seen my mother do."

Jasper sighed and stood up, looking at the stars. "I didn't even have the stars to keep me company in that thick bog. It was just me and those damned mosquitoes. Thousands and thousands of them. There were so many, that for a while, I really thought they might suck me dry. I hoped they would…

"It took me a while to realize that there was something about the mosquitoes that must have stopped me from turning into a vampire.

"I stumbled back into New Orleans, showed them I wasn't a vampire, and we set out to find out why. Three years later, here I am, traveling the world, hunting vampires and vampire hunters. If I find vampires, I kill them. If I find hunters, I show them how to protect themselves and give them the anti-venom."

"How many vampires you killed?" Adam's eyes were wide in the firelight.

Jasper shook his head. "Too many. Not enough. I don't know."

Adam gave him a puzzled look.

"The problem with killing vampires is … they used to be people. They used to be someone's mother, or brother. I caught up with my mother once. She begged me to kill her. I couldn't. She finally ran away, crying because she didn't want to hurt me. Somewhere trapped inside that monster was my mother."

Jasper met Adams's gaze. "Every time I kill a vampire, I wonder who's trapped inside of it. I wonder whose mother I killed."

"How sure are you this guy sold out your family?" Jasper looked at the ranch house through his spyglass. This time of year, the cattle were out in the pastures, so the corrals were empty.

"Sure as I can be without knowing for sure. Pa said Grindge was the big man out here until trade routes changed. He lost a fortune because of the Rail and Air War. Pa said he was even meaner now, trying to build his money back up."

"How does that make you sure he's the one?"

"Was a time he'd drive his cattle east to sell in Dodge City, but when the Santa Fe Railmen were all killed and the Santa Fe Railroad put out of business, Grindge had to go to Denver instead."

Jasper nodded. The Rail and Air War was a nasty business. After the Pinkertons got involved, hundreds of innocents were killed in the name of progress. In a battle to control trade routes, the Santa Fe lines had been bombed by airship and eventually abandoned as too expensive to repair.

"That meant Grindge had to drive his cattle through our land. He didn't bother to ask permission and trampled our crops. On account of the war, we had a new judge, one from back East somewheres that Grindge didn't have in his pocket. The judge ordered him to pay for the damages, but he never did. Then the judge disappeared and ain't been heard from since. Now, with my family gone, Grindge don't have to pay, and the land's as good as his."

They went back to looking at the ranch. Jasper counted a dozen ranch hands. There would be little chance of confronting Grindge in his own home.

"How often does Grindge go into town?"

Adam shrugged. "Pa only went once a month."

"Let's go find out."

"A mosquito machine? Really?" The Madam smirked. Her smoky voice matched the dark interior of the brothel. Her black hair, loosely bound up with a dark red ribbon, matched her salacious dress.

"Truly." Jasper nodded as he leaned against the bar and put on his best sales face. "It attracts the pests and draws them into the machine, never to be seen again. Imagine how happy your customers would be to be pest free during their visit at your fine establishment."

The Madam burst out laughing. A blush crept up Jasper's cheeks and burned his ears red.

"My apologies, Ma'am. I had no intention—"

The Madam reached over and tweaked Jasper on the cheek. "You are just absolutely priceless! What I wouldn't give to have more customers like you."

Jasper swallowed hard, glad he had left Adam tending to the wagon.

"I suppose you'd like to take trade for it?"

Jasper's ears burned a little hotter. "N-no, Ma'am," he stuttered.

"Awww ... Please?" The Madam leaned in close and revealed that her bodice was not laced tightly.

At a loss for words, Jasper fought to keep his eyes on the woman's face.

She took pity on him and leaned back, her voice becoming more professional. "Show me this machine. I don't much care whether or not my customers have mosquito bites, but my girls are certainly more appealing without them."

Jasper tipped his hat to her. "I shall fetch it from my wagon and return momentarily."

Still flustered, he headed outside, grateful for the chance to catch his breath away from the over-sexed woman.

At the wagon, Adam raised his eyebrows at the sight of Jasper's flushed features.

Jasper ignored him. "Hand me a mosquito machine, would you?"

Adam reached into a crate and pulled out a polished brass and copper contraption the size and shape of a loaf of bread. Jasper took it and pointed to smaller crate.

"Inside that one is the attractant. Would you hand me one of the phials out of there?"

"What'd you learn?" Adam asked as he handed over a delicate glass tube.

"Nothing yet. I have to keep up appearances. I can't just walk in there and ask if Grindge is here and whether or not he consorts with vampires."

"Why not?" The Madam's voice came from behind Jasper.

Jasper jumped and fumbled the equipment he was holding.

"Men ask me more direct questions than that all the time." The madam put a hand on her hip and cocked her head at him. "Is that really what you came here for?" She looked disappointed. "You were gonna sell me a fake toy just so you could ask about Grindge?"

"Uh, no Ma'am. It's not a fake ..." Jasper stammered.

Adam poked his head out of the wagon. The Madam looked up at him.

"Lord Sakes! Adam Timberlane! Is that you?" The woman stepped around Jasper to see better. "It is! I heard you were dead with your folks! Get down here, right now." She backed up so Adam could hop out of the wagon.

When he was down, she smothered him in a hug, pulling his head tight against her. "Lord Almighty! I cried my eyes out for you and your family." Her voice was shaky as her hands as they worried at his hair and tried to pull him even closer.

It was a long moment before she gained control of herself and held Adam away at arm's length to look at him. "Where have you been! What happened to you?"

Adam looked at the ground as though chastised. Jasper thought he saw similarities in the features of the boy and the woman.

"You two related?" he asked.

The woman shot him a sharp look.

"No." Adam shook his head. "Miss Elizabeth is a friend of my parents. Was a friend—" Adam gave into tears for the first time since Jasper had met him. Even in the stupor induced by the anti-venom he hadn't cried.

"Oh, Adam …" Elizabeth grabbed him again and pulled him close. "Thank God you're all right."

Jasper and Elizabeth looked down at Adam. Scrubbed clean and curled up in the soft bed, he looked like a small boy again.

"He's only twelve years old," Elizabeth whispered. "Big for his age. But he wasn't ready to handle that."

"No one is ever ready to handle their family being murdered by vampires," Jasper mumbled back.

"You sound as though you know."

"I do." Jasper turned to look at Elizabeth. "Tell me about Grindge. Adam thinks he could have set the vampires on his family to get the land. What do you think?"

Elizabeth looked out into the hall before shutting the door and closing them into the room.

"This is the first I've heard about vampires," she confided, "but I see the scars on Adam's neck, and the boy's not prone to telling tales. I think Adam's right. Strange things have been going on. The town's not talking about it, but the men who work for Grindge come in here, and they do. My girls are telling me Grindge has been buying up the ruined Santa Fe rail line, God knows why. But he's also collected the land from three families in the last two months. Adam's family is the third something has happened to recently. My guess is the other two were the same thing. The Sanderson family supposedly moved back East three months ago, but they didn't say goodbye to anyone except Elmore Grindge, when they supposedly sold him their land. Last month the Fitzpatrick family went missing. Just gone. Rumors about them being no good Irish running off to avoid paying their debts immediately started circulating, but they owed no debt to anyone I know of. Then Adam's …" Elizabeth's eyes filled with tears. "They burnt the house to the ground. Said it was Indians. We ain't had Indians out here in twenty-years. They don't want this blasted land back."

A sob shook her and Jasper felt compelled to put an arm around her. She buried her face in his shoulder. "He's my boy, you know. His momma was raising him for me. I was only thirteen, and I had nothing in the world."

The girl quietly slipped into the hallway, not quite shutting the door behind her. She was disheveled and partially undressed with her dress folded under one arm. "He's out," she whispered. "He drank a lot, too. I don't know if you'll even be able to wake him up."

"I'll handle it. Thank you." Jasper nodded to her.

Elizabeth smiled at her and waved her off. The girl hurried down the hall and disappeared through another door.

"Ready?" Jasper asked.

Elizabeth nodded and opened the door, pushing through before Jasper could object. Jasper followed and waited for his eyes to adjust to the dim light of the one low lantern in the room.

"We just need to wait for Cassie to tell the piano player to start up, then no one will hear him yelling," Elizabeth whispered.

Jasper turned his attention to the naked man in the bed. Grindge was a man who fit his name. His skin looked like the dirt was part of him. His long oily hair splayed around his head in clumped strands. And he snored like grinding gears.

When the music started, Jasper and Elizabeth each grabbed one of Grindge's wrists, intending to tie him to the headboard. Grindge was too drunk to notice.

"He won't be telling us anything tonight," Elizabeth said with disgust as she dropped his limp arm.

"And just what did you intend to ask him?" A rough voice came from the door way.

"Marshal Taylor!" Elizabeth jumped at the sight of the man holding a gun on them.

"So you figured that gave you the right to hogtie and torture the man?" The marshal had, for the moment, chosen not to arrest Jasper and Elizabeth. Although he appeared to have a relaxed appearance, Jasper could tell the man was still at the ready.

"It was my idea, Marshal." Elizabeth had been trying to deflect as much of the marshal's wrath as she could. She kept trying to place herself physically between Jasper and the marshal, but she was having a hard time in the tiny jail.

Grindge was sleeping off his drunk in the cell that took up half of the town's twelve by twelve foot jail.

Jasper kept his eyes down, looking properly abashed. His experience with lawmen was that they were either in on hunting the vampires from the beginning, or they were in the way. They never took well to vigilantes, even ones that hunted monsters, and Jasper didn't want to cross this man.

Marshal Taylor was short, but stout. Jasper got the impression Taylor could, and would, deal with a stubborn mule by throwing it over his shoulder and carrying it up the side of a mountain.

"How else were we going to get him to admit to consorting with vampires?" Elizabeth demanded.

"Did you ever think about coming to me?"

Elizabeth looked down, matching Jasper's demeanor. "After the last marshal ..."

"Well I ain't the last marshal, now am I?" Taylor turned and spit. His accuracy was better than most, and he made the spittoon cleanly. "I thought I was makin' headway in this town."

"I'm sorry, Marshal."

"You ought to be. If you'd have come to me, might be I'd have told you I already suspected vampires and was trying to find them myself."

Jasper looked up at the marshal.

Taylor nodded. "Yeah. I've got reports of over thirty people who headed for our town but never made it, or seemed to be here for one or two night before disappearing. Plus someone seems to be re-building the railroad at night, but no one knows who or ever sees them doing it. I know something's up, but nobody in this damn town talks to me!"

The day's heat was starting to radiate like a farriers' forge, making Jasper sweat as he sat in the little jail. He watched the unconscious form of Elmore Grindge through the cell bars, still sleeping off his stupor, and wondered how anyone could sleep in the heat.

A couple of Grindge's men had been by to collect their boss at sunrise, but the marshal chased them off. Jasper considered following them to see where they would lead him, but Taylor stopped him. Apparently Grindge's men were the last to see some of the missing people.

When Grindge woke up, he was so dehydrated from the heat and the alcohol his curses were unintelligible.

Jasper poured water for the prisoner. Grindge snatched at the tin through the bars, spilling half of it before quaffing the rest. As soon as he finished the water, he threw the cup at Jasper and vile expletives began flowing. He ranted for a full five minutes before he realized Jasper hadn't responded.

Grindge stopped shouting and took a breath, looking around and trying to assess his situation better.

"Do I know you?" he finally croaked.

"No. But unless you tell me where the vampires are, I'll likely be the last person you ever meet."

"Vampires! Ha!"

"I know you killed the Timberlane family."

"I didn't kill the Timberlanes! It was Injuns!" Even in his current state, the man managed an air of smug superiority.

"The boy lived. He saw you there." Jasper decided to lie and see what happened.

Grindge didn't react.

"If you don't tell me where the vampires are, I will bring in my team of professional vampire hunters and set up base in town. We'll put out the word that you hired us to come get rid of them. When word gets back to them, they'll come for you. After they kill you, we'll track them back to wherever they are."

Grindge laughed dryly. He managed a wicked grin and hissed through the bars. "You let me go now, and I'll let my men kill you instead of feeding you to the vampires."

A satisfied smile crept across Jasper's face.

"You son of a bitch!" Elizabeth dropped the food she had been carrying in as she heard Grindge's words. Flinging herself at the bars, she tried to punch and kick at the man behind them.

Marshal Taylor, who had been one step behind, pulled her off. "Can't get so close as to let him grab hold of you, Miss Elizabeth," he warned her.

"You wind it up by cranking the lever action, here, just like the .22 repeaters," Jasper handed the clockwork carbine to the marshal. "Each crank will get you a shot. Kill range is about fifty yards maximum. With the funnel filled full, you got fifty rounds."

Adam watched the men with big eyes.

Jasper tossed a pouch full of wooden marbles to the marshal. "These have all been fire hardened, blessed by a priest, and dipped in holy water. Aim for the heart. All you need is good penetration for a kill. If they're wearing armor of some sort, I've found an eye shot will take one out for at least five minutes, but it is most definitely not a kill. Never assume they are dead until you see the body start to decompose."

"God Almighty, son. You sound like you've done this before."

"I have."

Grindge snorted with disgust and muttered an obscenity. After a little persuading on the marshal's part, and seeing Adam for himself, Grindge had confessed to knowing the vampires were living in a mine.

The prisoner kept a keen eye on the boy, and Jasper wondered what it was Grindge thought he was going to get from Adam. Grindge never said anything though, and Jasper had other things to attend to.

"Vampires are sluggish during the day," Jasper continued. "As long as we stay on our toes, we'll be all right."

"I wish I could bring more men, but I can't take the chance any of them are under Grindge's thumb. There's only one I trust, and I need to leave him to tend the prisoner." Taylor had sent Elizabeth to fetch the man.

"I'm fine with that." Jasper handed him a leather case with a syringe full of anti-venom. "We'll be all right."

The mineshaft was cool, but the dust in the air was thick and stifling. Jasper and Marshall Taylor walked side by side, each carrying a clockwork carbine and a dim light.

"I can't hardly see by these safety lamps," Jasper cursed.

"Damn smart, using vampires to mine, if you ask me," Taylor muttered. "Stronger than normal men, can see in the dark, don't get killed by bad air … do they?"

Jasper chuckled. "I have no idea what bad air would do to them."

"Marshal? Jasper? Is that you?" Adam's voice faintly floated down the tunnel from behind them.

"Adam? I thought we told—"

"Grindge is comin'! They shot your friend! They're not more'n five minutes behind me!" Adam ran towards them, stumbling in the poor light.

The marshal held his lamp up high and looked down the dark tunnel where they expected to find vampires. "I'd say we're between a rock and a hard place."

Jasper glanced from the approaching boy and the danger behind him to the abyss below. "We need to kill the vampires first, eliminate the threat behind our back. Then we can sit in the dark and wait for Grindge's men, pick them off as they come in."

"They'll just trap us in here. Starve us out," the marshal cautioned.

"Do you have a better idea?"

"No. Let's go."

Adam caught up with them, looking frightened. "What're we gonna do?"

Jasper drew his revolver and handed it to Adam. "We're going to kill the vampires that killed your family, and then we'll deal with Grindge and his men."

They headed further into the mine, stumbling over loose rocks in the gloom.

A clinking noise echoed out of the dark ahead of them. Adam froze as both men readied their clockwork carbines in one hand while trying to hold lanterns in the other.

"I can't shoot like this!" Taylor hissed at Jasper as he switched the carbine to both hands and tried dangling the lantern from his fingers as he held the forestock.

"Don't worry," Jasper pushed on. "They'll be lethargic in the day. With luck we can kill them all before they wake up."

More chinking sounds came from ahead as Adam rushed to keep up, the pistol awkwardly held out in front of him.

"We're close," Jasper whispered. "Remember what I told you. Aim for the heart or the eye. Only a heart shot kills. They're not dead until you see them start to decompose."

Adam's breathing quickened into near gasps.

A quick movement ahead sent them all pointing their weapons at more jingling sounds. A vampire, pale as the moon, shielded his eyes from their lamp and curled into a ball on the ground, hissing in pain.

Jasper was quick with his carbine, aiming from the hip.

"Wait!" the marshal stopped him.

"We have to hurry, they will start waking up."

"Wait, dammit!" Taylor walked out in front of Jasper. "I know him! That's Earl Sanderson! Grindge said he moved back East three months ago."

The vampire seemed to react to his name being spoken, but still shrunk from the light.

"He is Mr. Sanderson!" Adam came closer. "I recognize him!"

"He ain't Earl Sanderson no more," Jasper warned. "He's dangerous."

"I thought you said they were still people in there." Adam's voice was accusing.

"I also said they were monsters. And we've got men coming up behind us, remember?"

"Why's he chained up?" Adam asked.

Jasper looked at the vampire's feet and saw shackles around the ankles. A chain passed through them and on into the dark. "What the hell …?"

Walking wide around the vampire, they followed the chain to another pair of shackles, on the ankles of another vampire. And another.

"It's a chain gang," the marshal muttered.

"Is this why they left me alive?" Adam's voice filled with horror. "They were going to do this to me?"

"That would explain how they captured so many vampires," Jasper shook his head. "Put them in chains before they turn…"

Jasper looked down at the vampire by his feet. A woman. No, a girl. Chained to the others and curled up against the pain of the light. She looked malnourished, even for a vampire. The vampire—no, the girl, started crying.

"I hear someone behind us," Adam whispered, his breathing ragged. "I think Grindge is here."

Jasper and Taylor looked at each other.

"We need to get deeper," the marshal said. "We need to get somewhere we can put out these lights so they can't see us, but we can see them coming."

Voices echoed down the tunnel from behind them.

Jasper set his jaw. "Let's go." He handed Adam the lamp and motioned for him to go ahead. "We need to find a side passage we can make a stand in. Hurry. We'll be right behind you."

Adam took off at a jog and the men followed, passing vampire after vampire chained together along the mine floor.

A shout came from somewhere behind them. A bullet struck the rock wall ahead of them, throwing sparks and whining away in ricochet before they even heard the sound of the report.

"Put out the light!" The marshal called to Adam as he dowsed his own. "They'll shoot at it!"

Adam stopped in his tracks, trying to blow out his lamp. Jasper and the marshal struggled not to run into him. Grabbing the light from Adam's hand, the marshal put it out as more bullets came at them.

Someone grunted in the darkness as a bullet found flesh.

"Who's hit?" Jasper groped where he thought Adam had been.

"Not me." Adam's voice was already farther down the tunnel.

"Wasn't me." The marshal was still at Jasper's elbow. "Must've hit a vampire."

"Keep moving." Jasper put his hand on the marshal's back in the dark and tried to follow by feel. "We've got to find some kind of cover."

"Jasper?" A voice rasped out of the dark. Even after all this time, and with so much pain in the voice, Jasper recognized it.

"Ma?"

"Keep going," her voice told him as the sound of chains began clanking in the darkness. "We'll stop them."

A light appeared at the edge of Jasper's awareness and he realized it was the lantern of one of their pursuers. As he continued into the darkness, he could see the silhouettes of the vampires rising and placing themselves between him and Grindge's men. First there were a handful of shadowy figures standing up, but as Jasper, Adam, and the marshal ran on, it became dozens.

Gunshots rang out behind them, but no bullets hit around them.

Ahead of them Adam yelped and went silent. The marshal stopped abruptly and Jasper ran into him.

"In here!" A voice hissed. Jasper felt hands pushing him, directing him into an alcove. He still had his hand on Taylor, and he recognized Adam's panicked breathing, but there was a press of bodies against him that did not belong to his little party.

"We'll protect you as long as we can." Another voice from the dark. "But, as we're all chained, it won't take them long to realize we can't reach them, but they can shoot us."

"Come here, lemme see." The marshal lit a match and Jasper found himself pressed into a small depression in the mine wall, surrounded by vampires. Adam's eyes were wide with terror.

"Standard fare," the marshal grunted as he examined a shackled ankle. He dug in his pocket and pulled out a key.

Jasper just had time to catch a glimpse of the key before the match burned the marshal's fingers and was dropped. He could hear the marshal fumbling with the key in the dark, trying to unlock the restraints.

"Allow me. I can see just fine," one of the vampires said.

In seconds, the sound of a clasp being released seemed to fill Jasper's world. It was followed by another, and another. The sound echoed in the darkness at regular intervals as the key was passed along. The excited hissing sound vampires make just before they strike began to fill the darkness.

Jasper knew the sound too well. Realizing he had lost his carbine somewhere along the way, he reached for his holster. Finding it empty, he began to fight panic.

Jasper jumped at the sound of the first scream.

"What in the hell…" Taylor's voice faded as realization set in.

Distant, the scream carried the agony of a painful death. It was followed by another, and another.

Jasper stepped back out into the main tunnel. There was no longer a press of bodies around him. Ahead, in the flickering light of a fire started by a broken lantern, he could see demons dancing through the flames and taking their due. He watched for a moment, unsure what to do.

In the gloom, he spotted his carbine on the ground. Jasper picked it up, put the safety lever on, and slung it over his shoulder.

A soft crying caught his attention. A figure huddling against the earthen wall.

"Ma?"

"Oh, Jasper …" she turned her face away so he couldn't see her. "This is all my fault. They used me. They knew I couldn't bring myself to kill people, and they used me to make more vampires."

<hr>

"You really think this will all work out?" the marshal looked across the candle-lit table at Jasper, Elizabeth, and the pale face of Jasper's mother.

"Every girl I've talked to feels it's better than whoring herself out," Elizabeth nodded seriously. "And we're going to get paid a damn sight better, too."

"What about the female vampires?" The marshal looked at Jasper's mother. "You gonna feed on whores too?"

"Most of the women suggested the opposite," she answered coolly. "Whoring themselves out for payment in blood from the customers."

Jasper tapped the mosquito machine sitting in front of him on the table. "With the anti-venom preventing the, uh, blood donors from becoming vampires and the sex all but free, I'm sure men will be lining up."

"And the youngin's?" Taylor pressed on. "What are they gonna do for food?"

"We'll buy blood from people for food." Jasper's mother's flat affect was menacing in its neutrality.

"Once we get word out to other vampires around the country," Jasper smiled at his mother and patted her pale hand, "we're hoping they'll all come here, to a safe source of food. Then there won't be any more killings and no more people turned into vampires. It'll be a boon to the town to have a

**86**

labor force of super coal miners. Production should be faster and cheaper than when normal men do the work. I'm sure the economic growth will attract attention and soon there will be a thriving market of people willing to sell their blood for money. I mean, how much easier can it be to get money?"

"And just exactly where is all of this money coming from?"

"Since Grindge is dead, and Adam is the only surviving human member of the families Grindge killed, we expect it's only right that Adam inherits the coalmine, the land, and the money Grindge stole." The look in Elizabeth's eye defied the marshal to argue to the point.

"The vampires will earn their pay in the coal mine, as real workers, not as slaves," Jasper assured him.

"Hmph!" Taylor grunted.

"What?" Elizabeth asked.

"How long do you think it will be before the vampires claim they deserve the same rights and privileges as everyone else?"

"Who's to say they don't deserve them?" Jasper asked.

His mother smiled, showing her pearlescent fangs.

# Colorado

# 1903

A chill ran down Orin Smith's spine. The mud showed the three-toed paw print clearly. He didn't even need to bend over to examine the bear track. It was bigger than his own handprint. He raised his eyes and nervously searched the tree line. He knew he was dealing with Old Mose.

He wondered if the rifle report he had heard first thing this morning had anything to do with the bear. Everyone had heard about Wharton Pigg and his obsession with catching the bear that killed Jacob Radliff, James Asher, and a couple more men. Stories of the men and livestock Old Mose had killed were commonplace in these parts, but Orin hadn't lent them any credence. All ranchers lost cattle and horses every now and then, but most folk blamed Old Mose.

Orin hadn't paid the stories no nevermind. Bears do what bears do. They weren't supernatural, smarter than men, or vindictive.

And yet, here were the three-toed tracks he had heard of.

Old Mose had lost two toes at the Stirrup Ranch a couple of years back when Pigg had put a trap out in waist-deep water where the bear had been known to wallow. Some said that proved the bear could be killed. Others said it just made him madder.

Looking up towards the tree line where the tracks led, Orin dismissed the superstitious thoughts. The truth was winter had come early this year, and it had stayed late. Spring was just beginning to show through and the animals were having a hard time finding the food they needed. He knew the bear must be hungry.

He suspected if he followed the tracks, he would find his missing cow, or what was left of it, partially eaten and half buried under a tree. The bear wouldn't be too far away. After hibernation, it wouldn't be able to eat too much at once, so it would stay close to the kill.

Unless the bear was already dead.

Perhaps Wharton Pigg was out here hunting Old Mose. Was it possible Pigg could have tracked the animal so soon?

Orin turned away from the tracks and went back to his horse, trying to decide if it was worth chasing down the grizzly, or even following the tracks to see if he found his missing cow. As he climbed into the saddle, he considered his new .30-30 Winchester repeating rifle in the saddle holster with a frown.

It was a mixed blessing. The rapid fire was a boon for hunting mule deer, or nearly anything else for that matter, but the smaller caliber made him hesitate at the thought of trying to bring down a big grizzly. Any grizzly.

Orin shook his head at his own gullibility. He didn't believe the stories that Old Mose, who'd gotten his name for just 'moseying' away when he was being shot with .50 caliber muzzle loaders, had been shot over a hundred times. More likely it was different grizzlies that got away after being shot.

He urged his horse forward with his knees, keeping her at a slow walk so he could watch the tracks and the tree line ahead.

His nerves getting the better of him, Orin drew his rifle out of the holster and laid it across his lap. The bear's tracks were fresh and bigger than any Orin had ever heard of.

The horse's ears perked and rotated to listen to the forest ahead. Not for the first time, Orin wished he could sense the things his horse did. He heard nothing. The damp leaves of last fall wouldn't rustle in the wind, and there were no crows or jays squawking in the trees.

Suddenly the day seemed too quiet.

Orin tried to shake off the feeling, but instead became

convinced he was being watched from the trees.

The horse nickered nervously, and he brought it to a stop. Watching where the horse's gaze led, Orin examined the shadows cast by the skeletal aspen trees and bare scrub oak bushes.

Nothing moved.

A heavy odor wafted under Orin's nose, just for a moment, and was gone. It was unmistakably the pungent smell of fresh blood.

Orin sniffed at the air, trying to catch the scent again. He had to be close to the kill site.

He turned the horse and urged it toward the closest trees, the direction the wind had come from. The horse laid its ears back as they moved forward.

The sun was beginning to warm the world and various scents filled the air. The earthy smell of the moldering leaves in the underbrush. The leather of Orin's own saddle and the musk of his horse. Then he caught the smell of blood again.

At almost the same time, he spotted a disturbed pile of leaves, scraped up to partially cover the heifer's corpse where it lay under a thicket of brush.

"Ho, there!" a voice called out from the trees.

The horse startled and Orin raised his rifle and scanned the woods.

"Up here!" A man bundled in furs sat in the crook of a large Aspen branch. He waved a mittened hand slowly in a friendly gesture.

When Orin spotted him, the man's bushy brown beard split into a toothy smile and he climbed down the tree with uncanny ease. The horse shifted nervously under Orin.

"If you are out looking for a lost cow, I've some sad news for you," the man said as he reached the ground. He adjusted his leather satchel and Orin noticed the muzzle loader slung across his back. Ragged scars scored the man's gaunt face and blood matted his hair above one ear.

Orin nodded without taking his eyes off the man. "I see that."

"Of course, if you are out looking for Old Mose, the news may be a sight better?" The man raised his eyebrows at Orin and looked at him with eyes so dark they were nearly black.

"No. Just my stock."

The man stepped forward jovially and offered his hand without removing the furred mitten. "Samuel Johnston."

Orin's horse stepped away from the man and Orin had to pull the reins to move closer again. Reaching down, Orin caught the man's hand and was taken aback at the vigorousness of the handshake. "Orin Smith." Samuel released Orin's hand just as the horse shied away again.

"My apologies if I'm trespassing on your land, Mr. Smith," Samuel said. "I knew this was the area Old Mose was last seen in afore winter so I started scouting it out when spring broke."

"Are you injured, Mr. Johnston?" Orin pointed to the blood running from Samuel's scalp and down his ear.

"What?" Samuel touched his head and seemed surprised when his fingers came away with blood on them. "Naw. I just must've scratched myself climbing up the tree."

"I thought I heard a shot this morning, about sunup. You get a bead on the bear already?"

Samuel shook his head. "Nope. I ain't seen 'im. I heard that shot, too, though. Thought for sure I'd find some feller waiting around here when I found the kill here." He pointed to the dead cow. "Seems like the perfect place to wait for a bear to come back."

"You a trapper?" Orin looked over the man's ragged clothing. It seemed to be entirely made of various furs.

"Was. 'Til Rendezvous broke up. Just kind of took to wandering after that."

"Rendezvous?" Orin frowned. "You mean where trappers used to sell their furs? There hasn't been a Rendezvous for over forty years."

Samuel's face darkened and he furrowed his brows. "Oh!" he laughed as he brightened again. "You thought I meant the old Rendezvous! Ha! I'm old, but I ain't that old. Give me a few more years, and then I might be, but not yet. Those were the days when men were men. Fighting out their existence one on one with Mother Nature."

Samuel looked back up at Orin with a lopsided smile. "Got a soft spot in my heart for those old timers. Grizzly bear did this to me." He pointed to the scars on his face. "Fended her off with a knife. Big ol' sow she was. If she'd been a boar, I wouldn't of stood a chance. It always made me feel like I knew what it was like for those old timers, out there in the world all alone.

Anyhow, look at me talk your ear off. My point was, if this land is yours, and you're wanting me to skedaddle, I'll go."

"You trying to catch Old Mose?"

"Eh. More just interested in seeing him with my own eyes. See if he's all they say he is. I've done a good share of trapping and hunting in my day. World's about trapped out. Nothing left to catch. I mostly just go my own way and do my own thing nowadays."

"If you're wanting to track Old Mose, I hear tell Wharton Pigg is the man to talk to."

Samuel snorted and looked away. "Forgive me. I've met the man. He couldn't track a horse across a plowed field. I daresay you've just tracked closer to Old Mose than he ever will." He nodded at the dead cow.

"What do you intend to do if the bear comes back here?" Orin asked.

"Oh, he'll be back. But, like I said, I just want to see him. What do you intend to do?" Samuel cocked his head at Orin.

Orin considered a moment. "I've really no interest in a grizzly. Don't need to see it, don't need to shoot it. But I don't really want it taking its pick of my calves all summer either. Do me a favor, if it comes back, shoot some powder off and scare it outta here."

"You don't want me to kill it for you?" Samuel scratched at his beard thoughtfully.

"If you're lookin' for a reward, I hear there's a five hundred dollar bounty on it."

"But you don't want it killed?"

"I ain't in no hurry to kill it. Just running it off is good enough. Everything's got to live somewhere."

Samuel nodded at him. "You sound like an Indian."

"Not Indian as far as I know. Just don't much care for killing when it's not warranted."

"Yup. Just like an Indian. Was a time they wanted to teach

the white man a lesson about hunting and trapping. Tried to show us the error of our ways. Damned if the white man didn't manage to show them first." Samuel seemed to lose himself in thought.

"You on foot?" Orin asked.

"Always. Don't know if you noticed or not, but me and horses don't get along so well."

"You're a long ways from the nearest town. When was the last time you had a hot meal?"

"A hot meal? Don't even remember what that is."

"If you're interested, my place is at the foot of the valley. Dinner will be ready around sundown."

Samuel grinned wide. "Much obliged!"

"Ho, there!" The call came from outside Orin's one-room house.

Orin sat down the knife he was sharpening and got up from the table. Careful not to hit his head on the low ceiling, he stepped around the only furniture in the room, his bed, a table, and three chairs, and opened the door.

The sun was just beginning to set as Samuel waved a mittened hand at him in greeting. His other hand held a skinned snowshoe rabbit by the ears.

"I brought something for your stew pot," Samuel called holding it up.

"Right kind of you. Already got beef stew with carrots and potatoes ready to eat, but that'll cook up nice for tomorrow. Come on in."

"Beef stew with carrots and potatoes. The hell you say! I can't remember the last time I ate a king's feast like that."

Orin grinned as Samuel entered the house, ducking so as to miss the low beams, and handed him the rabbit.

"I can't vouch for the biscuits though. I seem to be hit or miss with those," Orin said.

"Any biscuit softer'n a rock will go just fine with stew! You all alone out here?" Samuel looked around the inside of the house as he leaned his rifle against the wall and dropped his leather bag.

"For now. Got a wife and kid coming out from Kansas in a couple of weeks. I came out ahead last year to set up the ranch."

"I can see why you were out looking for your livestock then. Every head is important when you're first starting out. Hopefully the bear didn't hurt you none by culling that one."

"Not too bad. As far as I could tell, she wasn't pregnant. Likely she was sterile." Orin dropped the rabbit into a pot of saltwater next to the fireplace, to draw the blood out. "This'll make good eating. Thank you."

"No, thank you! Meager payment for beef stew and a warm fire."

Orin ladled out some stew into a bowl and put a biscuit on top. He turned to hand it to Samuel.

Samuel held out his mittened hands and hesitated. "Forgive me my manners. They are a bit rusty." He moved back to the door and dropped off his large fur coat into a pile on the floor, revealing a large barrel shape and broad shoulders and that Samuel was nearly thin to the point of malnutrition. Pulling off his mittens last, he tossed them on top of the pile.

Samuel returned and accepted the proffered bowl, cupping it in his hands and holding the warmth close to him.

Orin noticed Samuel was missing the last two fingers of his left hand.

"Oh, that smells heavenly. Bless you for sharing."

"Anytime. Did you get to lay eyes on Old Mose?"

"Did I ever!" Samuel sniffed at his biscuit and then dipped it into the stew before taking a bite. "Biggest damned thing I ever saw. Nine hundred pounds easy. And he just came out of hibernation! Probably hit twelve or thirteen hundred by the end of fall. That bear would put a bull moose to shame," he mumbled around another mouthful.

Orin filled his own bowl and sat down at the table. Samuel sat with him.

"That big?" Orin asked. "What'd you do?"

"Well, I let him eat some of the cow first, 'cause I figured no point in letting it all go to waste. Not to mention I didn't really think I could stop him. Then I jumped down out of the tree screaming like the devil himself." Samuel stopped eating and looked at Orin. "I'll tell you what. That bear wasn't the slightest bit scared of me. It went right on eating."

Orin frowned. "It really is a man-killer then."

Samuel shrugged and gulped down the rest of his biscuit. "He finally took off when I shot a wad out of my Hawkin. I see why they call him Old Mose, though. He still wasn't in no hurry. Walked out of there like it was his idea to go. He really didn't give me no nevermind."

Orin glanced at Samuel's rifle. The muzzle loader would take a skilled man, who was prepared, twenty seconds to re-load. "You emptied your rifle?"

"How else was I going to burn powder at him?"

"Weren't you afraid he'd come at you while you re-loaded? He's a man-killer!"

"Ain't we all if a man is shooting at us? He didn't want no part of me. He just wanted to be left alone. I don't reckon he'll be back around here to bother you again."

Orin watched the thin man awkwardly pick up and use a spoon with his three-fingered left hand while holding the bowl with his right. Samuel noticed him watching.

"Lost them to frostbite, my first winter out," Samuel said as he held up the hand. "Never without mittens now. Hard lesson learned."

"Samuel, if you don't mind me asking, how long you been traipsing around the mountains by yourself?"

Samuel paused with the spoon half-way to his mouth and thought before answering. "Couple of years, I guess. I haven't really been paying attention."

"What do you do? You said you don't trap no more."

Samuel chewed his food while he thought about it. "No. I don't trap no more. I quit that a long time ago. I realized that people was going to trap the animals clean out of the country, and they did. Can't hardly find a beaver no more. I spent some time trying to get folk to realize that, but they don't listen none. Besides, the mountains always call me back. I can't stay away for too long. So…I guess I kinda took to wandering. It's the only place that feels like home."

"Well, you're welcome to stay the night here, if you like.

96

Clean up. Get a good night's sleep by a warm fire."

Samuel looked at Orin with bright eyes. "That's right kind of you."

The sound of barking dogs woke Orin out of a dead sleep.

He had his boots on and his gun in his hand almost before he knew what he was doing. The dogs' cries intensified as Orin opened the door out to the early morning. Frosty air bit at his skin around the edges of his long johns. He ran around the corner of the house just in time to see a massive bear knock a leaping dog out of the air with an almost casual swipe of its paw.

Orin dropped to a knee and aimed his rifle at the bear, cranking a round into the chamber with a quick motion of his hand. His finger froze upon the trigger as he took in the enormity of the creature.

The dog hit the ground and rolled with a yelp, startled, but not hurt. The second dog dodged as the bear swung again with a seemingly half-hearted blow. Both dogs snarled and gnashed their teeth in frustration as the bear refused to let them get close enough to bite, yet didn't return their attack.

Living up to its name, Old Mose sauntered slowly towards the forest as the dogs edged closer, keeping out of the bear's reach.

"Hey!" Orin yelled at the retreating animals, not sure what else to do. He didn't know who the dogs belonged to. He still felt no desire to kill the bear. It obviously wasn't trying to hurt the dogs, and it wasn't threatening him.

The bear stopped and looked back at the sound of Orin's voice, ignoring the growling dogs. Standing up on its hind legs, it towered over him and the dogs.

Orin's eyes were wide as he guessed the bear stood fifteen feet tall.

It put one massive paw, a paw with only three claws, on an aspen tree with a trunk thicker then Orin's thigh. Giving an almost casual shove, the bear sent the whole tree crashing down. Frightened, the dogs yelped and cowered against the cabin.

The bear dropped back to all fours, eyed Orin with black eyes, and then slowly moseyed on into the forest without looking back.

It was several moments before Orin remembered he had a house guest and returned to the warmth of the building to check on him.

Samuel and his pile of furs he had slept on before fire were gone.

"We only missed it by half-an-hour!" Wharton Pigg called back to the men waiting outside Orin's house as he slapped his hat against his knee in frustration.

"You sure it didn't tree?" Pigg said turning back to Orin. "Bears are supposed to tree. Damned dogs are ruined." He continued without waiting for Orin's answer. "They tracked the monster here from where it killed Richard Welby, but they won't go any farther. Old Mose must've scared them but good."

"It killed someone?"

"Yeah, just up the valley there." He pointed toward where Orin had found Samuel waiting by the dead cow. "Richard Welby was two days ahead of us. We found him around sundown yesterday. He'd already been dead for at least a day. He claimed he knew where Old Mose was holing up for the winter. I guess he was right. Hell of a way to prove it though. He was torn to pieces.

"Hey! Is that his gun and pouch?"

Orin looked to where Pigg was pointing. Samuel's gun still leaned against the wall next to the leather satchel he had dropped. The bag had the initials RW stamped in it.

"Son of a…It is!" Pigg picked up the pouch. "Where'd you find them?"

Orin tried to find an answer for him, but his mind was working too hard.

"Were those your tracks we saw around the dead cow up there?" Pigg asked.

Orin nodded dumbly.

"You must've just missed seeing Welby's body. It was no more'n twenty yards from the cow. You're damned lucky the bear didn't get you, too. If our dogs hadn't got here and helped chase it off when they did, I bet it would've. That monster tracked you clear back to your house!"

Orin swallowed hard and looked back to the gun and bag Samuel had left. The bear hadn't tracked Orin back to his house. Orin had invited it to dinner.

## Wyoming Territory
## Near the Black Hills
## 1888

Even the flashes of lightning couldn't cut through the whirling storm, and if'n there was thunder, I couldn't tell over the howling wind and my chattering teeth. As I followed Uncle Pearl, his hurricane lantern kept flickerin' and I thought it'd go out for sure. The small yellow light it threw out ahead of us was so puny it felt like the wind was blowin' it away along with the straw and dirt. Already weak-kneed from fear, I stumbled as the whipping gusts pushed my feet out from under me, surely as any river would have.

Uncle Pearl caught me by the back of my shirt and lifted me up, like the barn cat carries kittens, until I had my legs again. He yelled something at me, but I could barely hear his voice, let alone make out the words. I did my best to keep on my feet and followed him the rest of the way to the barn, but all I wanted to do was run back to the house and hide.

I was scrawny for a ten year old and we all knew it. There wasn't anything I was going to be able to do to help out here, but I made the mistake of pointing out this storm was a lot like the one when my family had died. That was when Uncle Pearl said he needed my help getting the animals settled into shelter.

When we reached the barn, I was surprised none of the horses or cattle were waiting to get in. I wondered if they were already inside, hiding from the storm. I would have been.

Uncle Pearl bypassed the big alley doors and went to the small paddock door on the side. I could see the strain on his face in the dim light as even that door, in the force of the wind, tried to wrest itself away from him. He motioned me inside and I hurried past, into the darkness.

The relief on my ears was a godsend. I hadn't realized how loud the wind had gotten until it was no longer on me. I was shaking near uncontrollably.

Uncle Pearl's lantern filled a small area around me as he came in, the door slamming shut behind him with a wood splintering crash. He held his light high. There were no animals inside.

"Light the lamps." He nodded at me. "I'm going to get rope. I reckon we need to tie doors open in this wind, or someone's likely to get killed."

By someone, I knew he meant me. I did my best to not think about it, or how much this really was like the night I lost my family.

With palsied hands, I went to work. Grabbing strike-anywhere kitchen matches from inside the old tin can nailed to the wall, I made the rounds to all six lanterns on the large posts. Pressing the little metal arm that lifted the glass globe up an inch, I stuck matches in and lit wicks. I was glad I had just filled all the lanterns yesterday. If I'd had to do it now, while I was all fumble-thumbs, I'd likely broken half the globes and spilt all the coal oil.

As I made it to the last lantern, the soft thumps of things hitting the outside of the barn changed to a stronger, steadier sound, and I knew the rain had finally broke.

"Paul!"

I lowered the last globe back down, finished with my task. "Yes, Uncle Pearl?"

"You run back to the house, get the girls and get into the potato cellar! Tell your Aunt Vernona I said a twister is comin'. I feel it in my bones."

Any relief I might have felt at being allowed to get out of the storm was wiped away when Uncle Pearl said "twister". A lump rose in my throat. Not again.

"Paul!"

"Yessir?" Uncle Pearl was standing there with ropes over his shoulder and a lantern in his hand. He looked a lot more like Pa than I'd ever realized. And a lot like Pa had the last time I'd ever seen him.

"You get in there with 'em, and you stay there, hear me? Make sure they're safe."

"Yes sir." I spun on my heel and ran, fast as I could go, out of the barn and back into the raging storm. I didn't dare look up at the sky.

What if I saw them again? What if they came again?

The house lights were a beacon I could easily follow on a calm night and the path was a well-worn one I had traveled many times, but as the icy rain pummeled the side of my head and poured into my eyes I lost my direction, slipping and falling in the mud like a wallowin' pig.

Every step I put down, every hand that went into the mud, I imagined I felt the squirming again. My heart pounded uncontrollably. I was panicking, but I couldn't help it. Tears burned hot on my face in the cold rain and I tried not to wail like a baby. I imagined I could hear my brother screaming over the noise of the rain. I waited for the burning feeling of those sucking bites …

The next thing I knew, I was running for the hill the cellar was built into. All I could think about was flinging myself into the comforting blackness of the room hollowed out of the side of the small hill.

It would be cool and quiet, just like always.

The rain turned hard as stone as hail began pelting me, bringing me to my senses even as I sprawled into the mud again. My cheeks burned with shame as I realized I had been too scared to go tell Aunt Vernona. Just like last time…

I threw my hands over my head to protect myself as more hail fell. Fear got me to my feet as the hail fell. Just like last time…

It was only the turning of my head, to protect my eyes as I got up, that allowed me to see the quick flicker of light out in the pasture. Another flicker and I saw two unfamiliar faces in the dark. I looked back to the barn and saw Uncle Pearl still moving inside. My throat constricted. Rustlers! They were using the cover of the storm to steal livestock!

I climbed to my feet, torn with what to do.

I tried to go back to the barn and warn Uncle Pearl. I swear I did. But my legs wouldn't move that way.

Another chunk of hail hit me, a bigger one this time, and my body took a mind of its own, running. It was all I could do to make myself run for the house and not the potato cellar. My bare feet slipped so badly in the mud, I finally left the path and risked the rocks hidden in the weeds. Cold hailstones separated my toes and jabbed the bottoms of my feet. A barrage of hail nearly drove me to my knees. Welts were already rising.

I twisted my ankle on something I imagined was a hailstone big enough to kill me had it found its mark. Fear spurred me on and I reached the house at full speed. Trying to stop, I slid out of control into the porch, gaffing my shins and tumbling into the door with a crash.

"Good Lord!" Aunt Vernona cried out at me as I burst into the house. "Paul! What on Earth—?"

"Rustlers, Aunt Vernona!" I had to yell over the noise of the hail on the roof. "I saw lights out in the field! Uncle Pearl don't know! He sent me back 'cause there's a twister comin' but it ain't just a twister! This is just like last time! We gotta get in the potato cellar!"

Aunt Vernona stood straight, smoothed her skirts, and threw her shoulders back like she does when she won't brook no arguments from Uncle Pearl. "Get the rifle." She pointed at the Henry in the corner.

I didn't move. I was too panicked.

"Paul. You mind. Now!"

I jumped. I didn't much like the rifle. I barely had long enough arms to use it and it wouldn't protect us from what was coming anyways. I'd seen Pa empty everything he'd had…

But I did what I was told. When I turned around, Aunt Vernona was holding Uncle Pearl's Colt and checking to see if'n it was loaded.

"Ellie, May. You two each grab a blanket, hold hands, and follow Paul to the potato cellar. No dawdling!"

My two younger cousins, who had been sitting with hands over their ears, were old enough to understand the tone of voice. They moved quickly, grabbing blankets from the bed in the corner of the small room. Aunt Vernona had to help May gather her blanket up enough to carry it. When she finished, Aunt Vernona put out all the lamps but the hurricane lamp by the door, which she picked up.

"Paul, you lead the way. Keep your eyes open. Watch for your Uncle."

I swallowed. I didn't want to go back out into the storm. There were worse things out there than rustlers, and I knew it, even if no one else believed me.

"Paul."

I nodded. The potato cellar was the only place safe.

The Henry was clumsy in my arms and I fumbled opening the door. Wind slammed the door into me, knocking the rifle barrel into my nose. Blinding pain, smelling of cold iron and gun oil, flashed into my eyes.

Wincing I checked my nose for blood.

Aunt Vernona had a concerned look, but nodded me on. "This is no time to be a baby, Paul."

I steeled myself and went out into the dark and the pounding hail. The hail prevented me from looking up into the blackness of the sky, looking for things in the night, so I kept my eyes on my feet.

Dim light shone from behind. Aunt Vernona was holding the hurricane lantern high, trying to get light out ahead of us. The girls held their blankets over their heads, shielding themselves from the hail.

We were fortunate to have our cellar built into a hill, rather than dug out of the ground. Aunt Vernona once told me she and Uncle Pearl had picked this spot for the house just for that reason. As I struggled to open the heavy wooden door against the wind, I realized how much easier it was for me to open than it had been for Pa to open the one built into the ground under our house...

Protecting my throbbing nose from the rifle barrel, I put my back to the door, bracing it open so everyone could get in.

As the lantern passed me, I noticed blood on my hands and all over the gun. Aunt Vernona noticed it too.

We moved inside and the wind slammed the door shut, knocking me over as I tried to get out of the way. Aunt Vernona threw the small sliding lock to bar the door against the wind, then grabbed the storm brace and set it against the door. When she was done, she held the light up to my face.

"I think you broke it." She grimaced. "Let me see…"

"You're bleedin', Paul!" May, dragging her wet and muddy blanket on the earthen floor, pointed at my face.

"You two get all the way in the back," Aunt Vernona told the girls. "Make a bed with the blankets and lie down."

Ellie tugged at May's shoulder and they went to the back with the few apples and potatoes left from last year.

I tried to hold still as Aunt Vernona reached out for my nose. I'd seen my Pa get his nose set after breaking it. It looked like it'd hurt like the dickens. I shook as she put her hands to my cheeks, turning my head so she could see.

"It's straight. We'll need to check it again tomorrow." She kissed my forehead.

I sighed with relief. I was finally in the cellar. Last time, the cellar was the only place there weren't—

There was rhythmic pounding on the door.

"Get the rifle, Paul." Aunt Vernona pointed to where I had leaned it against the wall.

I grabbed it as she pulled the Colt from her apron pocket.

Aunt Vernona pulled out the storm brace, slid the wooden latch and pushed against the door to open it. Uncle Pearl stepped into the light, a grim look on his face. A pistol glinted behind him, and he was followed in by two men I didn't recognize. They both held guns on Uncle Pearl.

"Don't do it!" The first man turned his gun on me.

"Drop it." The second man was in the light now and his gun was pointed at Aunt Vernona.

My arms were shaking and the barrel dipped and rose. I looked at Uncle Pearl to see what I should do, but he was looking at Aunt Vernona. He nodded at her.

She slowly laid the Colt on the ground. I did the same.

The first man kept his gun pointed at my face. I felt a throb in my broken nose and thought I knew where the bullet would hit if he pulled the trigger. Tears welled up in my eyes as my breath got short.

"Move back," he waved the gun at me. His long stringy blond hair was matted to the sides of his head and beaded water shone on his bald spot. He held his hat in his other hand.

I moved away, my legs jerky and stiff with fear, unable to take my eyes off the gun pointed at me.

"Hey! Ain't you that kid what had that old injun at the general store talkin' about Thunderbirds?" He kept his gun aimed at my face for a moment longer, then lowered the barrel.

"Mama, who's that?" May's voice came out of the darkness behind us and the other man's gun snapped to her.

"Don't you dare point a gun at my daughter!" Aunt Vernona stepped in front of May. "I don't care what you want, don't you dare point a gun at them!"

The man's scowl almost softened, his wild, bushy mustache drooping, but the other man shoved Uncle Pearl towards Aunt Vernona. "Everyone back up and give us some room!" The man with the mustache waved his gun back and forth. Aunt Vernona put her hand on my shoulder and pulled me backwards.

Something hit the door, hard, and made us all jump.

May started crying, and I could hear Ellie trying to soothe her.

"Charlie, take the lamp and go see if'n you can find Merle 'n Nate."

The man with the stringy hair made a sour face but put his hat on his head and reached out a hand to take the lantern.

Uncle Pearl took it from Aunt Vernona and stepped forward to hand it over. "We don't want no trouble —"

"Well you goddamned got it!" The first man raised the barrel of his gun to Uncle Pearl's face. Aunt Vernona pulled me closer, her arm squeezing me tight enough to hurt. She moved backwards, closer to Ellie and May, and dragged me with her.

"Take it easy, Jasper! We din't come here to kill no one." Charlie took the lantern and backed away from Uncle Pearl, but his eyes were on Jasper.

"That was afore they seen our faces! Now shut up and go find Merle and Nate!" I couldn't tell if Jasper was yelling to be heard over the storm or because he was angry. It didn't matter. His eyes said he was going to kill us.

My knees began shaking again, and I was afraid I was going to fall down. I had a horrible thought, and just for a moment, wished it was that night, and that these rustlers would…

Charlie holstered his pistol and took his hat off again before slipping behind Jasper and putting a shoulder against the door to push it open. It didn't move.

I didn't want it to move. I'd rather have kept them in there with us. I didn't want what might be out there to get in.

He grunted and pushed harder, managing to get the door to wiggle.

"Unlatch it, dumbass!" Jasper yelled over his shoulder.

"I did!"

Jasper moved back and helped Charlie push. The door fought back as the wind roared outside.

Some part of me hoped he would get out and…

The wind went quiet.

I could feel it. It was happening again.

The two men finally pushed the door open far enough for Charlie to squeeze out.

"What in the hell…?" Charlie held the lantern so he could see.

Even in the dim light, I recognized my favorite milk cow, Dandelion. She had a pattern on her hide like the jagged leaf of a dandelion. Her body was lying on the ground in front of the door, blocking it. She looked like she'd been shot, over and over again—until I spotted the hailstones in the wounds.

My ears popped.

Jasper took the lantern away from Charlie and looked down at the cow. "Goddamn!" he swore. "There's gotta be a goddamn twister out there! Shut the door!"

Even as he and Charlie tried to pull the door shut, it fought them. Dandelion seemed to slowly float up into the air and drift away.

"Dear God in Heaven..." Charlie's feet left the ground too, and he scrambled to find something to hold on to.

I watched wide-eyed as he grabbed desperately at Jasper, then caught hold of the storm brace. It wasn't attached to anything and lifted up in his hands, light as a feather, as if Charlie was some kind of magic flying fairy who made things weightless with a touch. The shock was wide on his face when he disappeared in the blink of an eye.

He was there, then he wasn't. He'd been sucked out so fast, I wasn't even sure I'd seen him go out the door.

Next I knew, Uncle Pearl was knockin' me and Aunt Vernona to the ground, pushing us back to where Ellie and May were huddled in their blankets. "Stay down!" he yelled at us.

Out of the corner of my eye, I saw Jasper trying to run for us as he seemed to float up into the air, too. Then he, and the lantern he was holding, was gone.

The storm raged in the darkness, louder'n anything I'd ever heard. Even louder than last time. Like ol' Nick hisself was mad at the moon. Aunt Vernona and Uncle Pearl held on tight to me and Ellie and May, and we all stayed as far back in the cellar as we could. I could feel the wind suckin' at us, like it was hungry.

Then the real noise started.

Lord up in Heaven, the storm was loud. It was like standing too close to a train going by at full speed. But then the world boxed my ears.

I'd had my ears boxed by a general store owner who'd thought I stole a piece of candy. It hurt bad. But he'd only done it once. The storm started pounding my ears over and over again.

I covered my ears with my hands and screamed. It didn't help.

In a lightning flash, I saw my cousins crying and holding their ears, but I couldn't hear them. In another, I saw the cellar door, as if possessed by a demon, slamming back and forth impossibly fast, each time another hammer blow to my head.

The banging went on until I couldn't think of anything but the noise and the pain in my ears. I curled into a ball, holding my head and crying.

I don't know how long the pounding noise had been gone when I finally realized it. Seconds to hours, I couldn't tell. I took my hands off my ears and sat up.

Dimly, I heard my cousins crying. Everything was so muffled, it was like I had my fingers in my ears.

"…all right?"

Uncle Pearl was talkin', but he sounded far away.

"Paul!" Uncle Pearl called.

"Yes, sir?" I answered back, my own voice distant and strange.

"Where are you?"

"Right here." I felt in the darkness towards the last place I knew he'd been. A strong hand caught me by the wrist and pulled me closer.

I felt Aunt Vernona wrap her arms around me and Uncle Pearl's big hand muss my hair.

"Oh, thank God!" I heard Aunt Vernona's voice. I could tell it was right in my ear, but it didn't sound like it. More like she was in a different room.

She let go of me, and I knew she was comforting Ellie and May.

"Can anyone still hear the storm?" Uncle Pearl's asked.

No one said anything, so I spoke up. "I can't hardly hear at all. I feel like when Mr. Womack boxed my ears, but worse."

"It was the door," Uncle Pearl said. "The twister was banging it…"

I couldn't tell what else he said. I could still hear my cousins crying, but I couldn't make out anything other than that.

One of my cousins' little arms grabbed at my leg. I didn't know which one it was, but I figured if their ears hurt like mine, they must both be pretty scared. I reached down, searching in the dark for a hand to hold.

What I found felt like an arm, but wet and squishy.

I let go in a panic and my heart crawled up into my throat. Please God, don't let it be…

I scrambled away.

It had been big enough I thought it had been an arm at first… Maybe last time I would have thought that, thought that it had been smashed horribly, thought the wetness would be blood…

I tried to wipe the slime off my hands, but it wouldn't come off. I got to my knees, still trying to get it off, when I felt the first sucking, burning bite on my foot, I screamed.

"There not supposed to be in here! It's supposed to be safe in here!" I could hear my voice, high and shrill, but it didn't sound like me. I was up and kicking wildly in the dark. I knew one had bitten my foot—it felt just like before.

There had to be more. There were always more.

"Paul? What are you going on about?" Uncle Pearl's voice.

"They're in here! The worms are back!" I kicked something.

Aunt Vernona cried out and I felt her rise up next to me. I hadn't meant to kick her, but I couldn't help myself.

"Nona?" I heard Uncle Pearl ask.

"I'm fine," she called back.

And then she screamed.

Even deaf as I was, it was a piercing shriek.

"Pearl! Pearl!"

"I'm right here! What's wrong? Nona? What's wrong?"

I stepped on something that squished and rolled under my foot and I fell.

"Pearl! Get the girls!"

My hands and face landed on the same wet, mushy thing I felt before. And it moved.

It writhed under my touch, like a giant snake, and I screamed as I felt another burning bite on my arm. Stumbling to my feet, I fell backwards again, landing on someone.

Uncle Pearl's hands moved over me, finding the collar of my shirt, just as he had in the storm, and pulled me to my feet. He let go, leaving me standing next to him.

I was still screaming.

"Take May!" he cried as he put my littlest cousin into my arms.

May, still crying, wrapped her little arms and legs around me.

Losing my balance, I stepped back. My heel landed on something slimy that moved sickeningly under my bare foot.

Lightning flashed. For just a moment I could see Uncle Pearl, holding Ellie in his arms, and Aunt Vernona holding them both tight—and I could see the worms.

As big around as Ellie's arms, and as long as Uncle Pearl's legs, they were coming out of the cellar's earthen floor all around us. One was sucking at Aunt Vernona's leg.

May saw them, too. She buried her face in my neck and screamed.

I screamed with her. They weren't supposed to be in here! Not in the cellar! Last time, the cellar was the only place I was safe!

"Out!" Uncle Pearl yelled. He didn't have to tell me twice.

I stumbled and tripped over slimy, twisty things in the dark as I headed out of the cellar. They squished and rolled and moved disgustingly under my feet.

Holding May tight, I stumbled out into the night, eyes immediately going to the sky, searching for the terror I knew must be coming.

Stars shone brightly in half the sky. The storm was moving away from us, distant lightning flashing gold under clouds too dark to be lit up. In the opposite direction, I could see the dark outline of the Black Hills against the sky.

And the worms. So many more than the night my family had died. Slimy pale skin glistening in the starlight, their squirming made the ground ripple like pond water. And more were coming out of the ground even as I watched.

But something was missing.

A familiar outline was gone.

There was no barn.

I turned for the house. It was gone, too.

"Paul?" I heard Aunt Vernona behind me.

Turning back I could see her and Uncle Pearl and Ellie coming out of the hillside cellar.

Worms were squirming around at their feet

"There's no place to go!" I screamed. "The barn and the house are gone! We gotta get under cover before they come!"

May snapped her head off my shoulder to look up. "Where?" she asked, moving her face back and forth in front of mine, trying to see around my head.

I took no joy in knowing someone finally believed me. It was too late.

"Paul!" Uncle Pearl called from behind me.

"We have to run away! They're coming!" I screamed and carried May as fast as I could.

"Stop!" Aunt Vernona cried.

"Run!" I continued away from the cellar as more and more worms came out of the ground around it, and from inside. My aunt and uncle still didn't understand. They might believe me, now, but they still didn't understand. I couldn't do anything to help them but hope they followed me. If nothing else, maybe I could save May.

I kicked a worm out of my way as I ran. The first time I had seen them, I was sure they were just big old earthworms, and I had laughed for being afraid of them. That was before they had started biting.

One managed to bite my calf as I went by. I ignored it. They weren't what I was afraid of. I glanced up at the sky just in time to see the dark silhouette that froze my soul with terror.

Then it was like another twister hit, sending me spinning through the air, holding desperately onto May so I wouldn't lose her. I couldn't lose her. I had to save her.

We landed in mud and slid to a stop. May was silent, wide-eyed and staring me in the face, and I realized I was holding her so tight she couldn't breathe. I relaxed my grip and she gasped, too shocked to cry.

Ellie screamed. May and I both looked. Another dark shadow swooped in front of Aunt Vernona and Uncle Pearl, blocking my view of them, for just an instant, and then it was gone. I could see them falling down, landing among the squirming worms, and, in-between us, dirt clods and mud rained back down to the ground, back to a bare place where the soil had been rent and the worms had been taken.

I looked up and saw more dark shapes, circling overhead in the night sky.

They were even bigger than I remembered. As I watched, another dove towards us. May shrieked. I could see the gleaming of its sharp beak and outstretched talons. It grew impossibly big, big as the side of a barn, then, at the last possible moment, it pulled up, hitting only the top of the ground with its claws and taking away with it earth and giant worms.

The force from its wings blew May and I over, sending us rolling away in the mud.

I scrambled to my feet, did my best to scoop May up, and then I ran. I didn't know where I was going, but I half-carried, half-drug her as fast as I could. We had to get away from the worms before one of the birds decided to try us. Because that is how it had all happened last time.

I was the only one who had gotten away.

I stumbled through the dark, the ground unfamiliar now that all of my landmarks were gone. I had no idea which way I was going, other than away. Whooshing sounds, muffled in my damaged ears, happened all around us. I heard Ellie scream, and maybe Aunt Vernona, but I didn't stop. I had to get May away.

I hit something hidden in the weeds and May and I fell. This time, when I pulled my hands away from the slimy wetness, there was enough starlight I could tell it was blood. But I hadn't needed to see it. I could smell it.

We were sprawled over the freshly dead body of one of the cows, the thick musk of its fear and blood hung around it like a fog. Three worms were feeding on it.

May screamed and I pulled her off, still moving away from the cellar. There were not so many worms here, but a gust of wind behind me proved we were still too close to the giant birds.

"Paul!" May pointed as I tried to pick her up again. "Look! It's the roof of our house!"

Near as I could tell, it was the roof from the porch, raised up a bit, propped up by a broken off support beam.

"Get under it, May. Crawl under, and we'll hide there." There were few enough worms here I decided it would be better to fight them than be out in the open. I waited for May then followed her in. When we settled, I had a good view of where we had come from.

I couldn't see any sign of anyone else, but we were close enough to count the worms feeding on the cow. We watched three more crawl up and join the feast.

Then, in the blink of an eye, the cow vanished.

A single worm fell back to the earth with a wet thump. Dirt and weeds rained back down from the sky. The bird had taken the cow so fast May and I never had the chance to scream.

We drifted off to sleep sometime in the night, watching the giant shadows rise and fall from the sky, filling claws with wriggling worms.

The sound of May yelling woke me.

"Mama! Mama!"

Blinking my eyes open, I saw her running away from me. The sky was just starting to lighten. The events of the night came back to me and I realized where I was. Fear seized my heart again.

I had been here before. I had seen this before.

But May was all right. I knew that. Tears burned my eyes. At least I had saved her.

"Mama!" Her voice was sweet to my ears. And it was so good to be able to really hear again. Things still sounded funny, but I could hear.

Then I heard Aunt Vernona's voice and my tears broke free like a dam had let go. We weren't alone. Not this time.

As I crawled out, I heard Uncle Pearl and Ellie.

"Paul's over here!" May called.

I stood up and looked around at the green grass for as far as I could see. All the way to the Black Hills. Rising up over them, the sun was bright and warm.

There was evidence of the night, if I looked for it. Torn up mud in front of the cellar and where the house used to be, where the barn had been. Other than that, I was lookin' out at

God's Green Earth with my aunt, uncle, and two little cousins running towards me with relief on their faces.

It's hard to believe God could follow a night like that with a bright, sunshiny day. But he had, just like he did last time. I supposed some folk like to take that as a sign that everything is all right now. But I knew better. It's just a fresh coat of paint on what's already there.

# California
# 1851

T"he Dead Moon." The Indian's voice was emotionless. His strong features were outlined with blue and gold light as he looked up past the campfire and into the moonlight. "We should not be here."

"No more gods of the winds out of my ass bullshit! I can't take it no more!" The expedition's white guide, Crawley, no longer bothered to hide his disdain for the local Indian guide. He stood, slapping dirt off his buckskin leggings with his fur hat as he stormed off into the night. "Brave Elk my ass. Your name ought to be Whining Dog!"

A couple of the men around the second campfire, less than fifteen yards to the south, heard the outburst and laughed boisterously. They were quick to repeat the insult to the other half-dozen who had not heard.

Jonathon Thomas Jefferson, left alone at the smaller fire with Brave Elk, watched the bitter mountain man disappear into the darkness of the forest. Brave Elk, still watching the moon, did not react to Crawley's harsh words or the men's laughter. Glancing up at the moon, Jefferson saw no difference tonight from any other. He waited, knowing the Indian would explain himself when he was ready.

The men around the other campfire continued to toss random jibes. Not directly aimed at Brave Elk, they were certainly for him to hear. Jefferson considered reprimanding the men but knew it would do nothing but foster more hostility.

"All will die if you do not turn back," Brave Elk finally stated. He slowly turned his gaze to Jefferson. "This railroad you search a path for cannot go this way. There is no reason for us to continue this way."

"Even if the rails can't go this way, I have to map it to show that it can't."

"I cannot lead you any farther in this direction."

Jefferson sighed. This was not completely unexpected. Brave Elk was not the first Indian guide to abandon the expedition. The Indians all seemed to have a range outside of which they would not travel.

"I understand. You must do what you must," Jefferson met the Indian's gaze, "and I must do what I must."

Brave Elk contemplated that for a moment. "You are a good man, Jefferson. You treat people as people and not as animals and things to be used." His stoic face turned meaningfully toward the darkness where Crawley had disappeared. "You gave my family payment, in case I did not return. I cannot lead you farther, but I will not abandon you. If you are to continue, you should have knowledge of the death that awaits you. The death that awaits us."

One of the horses tied to the highline nickered quietly in the dark. Jefferson glanced at them, noticing their dark eyes reflected the two campfires ominously. The animals all seemed to be looking at him.

"Ahead, in the direction you seek to travel," Brave Elk continued, "lies the Land of the Giants and the entrance to the First World. The world the People came from. The Spirits still move back and forth between the Worlds, but the People do not. We cannot. The Spirits will not allow us. We were cast out and our punishment is that we cannot return. If we come too near, we will be killed."

Similar to many legends Jefferson had heard from many peoples, the story did not forestall him. "I understand. You don't have to come with us."

"I am not a 'whining dog'. I will come with you. When you see, I will do my best to bring you back alive."

"Jefferson."

The sound of Brave Elk's whisper caused Jefferson to look up from where he kneeled with a compass and sketch book. The Indian had refused to scout or lead, but he had not left Jefferson's side since their discussion at the campfire last night.

"Do you see the elk, behind the trees?" Brave Elk kneeled beside him and gestured subtly with his head. His tone of voice indicated he did not want to raise the attention of the other men, who were off their horses for a toilet break.

Jefferson looked and spotted the large animal standing among the trunks of the ancient trees. He nodded silently.

"Do you see his antler is broken, at the top?"

He nodded again.

"That elk is my Spirit Guide. He has come to warn us. We should turn back."

Jefferson must have taken too long to answer, so Brave Elk offered more.

"See the antler? It has been that way since I was a boy. That is how I recognize him."

The elk was one of the biggest Jefferson had ever seen, with a large rack, wider than a man could spread his arms. The top of the left side was broken off, unbalancing the symmetry by almost a foot.

"Elk shed and regrow antlers every year." Jefferson wondered if Brave Elk thought he wouldn't have known that.

"Then you understand how I recognize my Spirit Guide."

A thunderous *CRACK* broke the quiet moment and the elk fell backward into the thick brush.

A wild whoop sounded through the trees. "We eaten' good tonight!" Crawley proudly tramped back out from the bushes, one hand holding his still smoking rifle and the other holding up his buckskin pants.

"Jesus, Crawley," Hart, a small man with a pronounced limp, called out. "Which rifle'd you shoot him with?"

Raucous laughter broke out among the men, and Crawley beamed out from under his fur cap as he headed toward his kill.

Jefferson stood, not sure what to say to Brave Elk, but the Indian put a hand on his arm, holding him in place.

Crawley gave up trying to walk while holding his pants up and stopped to lay his rifle down and tie his breeches. Two of the men, a rowdy red-bearded man named Rutger and Smythe, a man Jefferson thought could be the greasiest person he had ever met, laughingly bounded past Crawley, excited at the prospect of fresh meat.

After a moment, Rutger called out from the brush, "Hey, Crawley! Next time don't get so excited you take your pants down. You missed."

"Bullshit!" Crawley finished with his pants and scooped his rifle up out of the dry grass. "I ain't never missed!"

Jefferson glanced at Brave Elk. Crawley hadn't missed. Jefferson had seen the elk fall backward.

Brave Elk dropped his hand from Jefferson's arm, put on a disinterested expression, and knelt back down to look at the map Jefferson had been sketching.

* * *

"I got 'im!" Mayer whooped as the echo of the shot still hung in the air. He pulled his horse out of line and headed toward his kill. "See, Crawley?" Mayer grinned, showing his tobacco stained teeth. "That's how you do it!"

Jefferson stopped his steed and turned to look back. On the side of the hill, behind and to the side of the group of men, he spotted movement. The elk, wounded, was loping slowly into the rugged terrain and away from the men.

"You mean that's how you make getting dinner into hard work," Crawley answered from in front of Jefferson as he turned his horse to join the chase.

Brave Elk pulled his horse alongside Jefferson's. "They will not catch up. It will always stay just far enough ahead to keep them following."

Jefferson watched as Crawley, Mayer, Tamp, and Dex rode out after the wounded animal. He had learned a long time ago that the best way to control men was to let them do what they wanted when it didn't really matter.

* * *

Giving up trying to scout and draw his map at the same time, Jefferson called camp early. Without Crawley or Brave Elk scouting the trail ahead, he had been forced to backtrack often, costing time he would rather have devoted to marking his map. Brave Elk stoically remained at his side, but would not lead.

"I reckon stopping was a good idea." Rutger offered an unsolicited opinion as he scratched at his red beard. "They would've caught up by now if we hadn't been riding in circles." He glared at Brave Elk as he spoke.

Jefferson ignored the barb, but he knew the men resented his moving on without Crawley. Jefferson was the lead of the expedition, but Crawley was boss as far as they were concerned.

Dismounting, Jefferson walked back to his personal mule and fished around inside one of the packs until he pulled out a bottle of whiskey. "Rutger!" He called the man over and handed him the bottle. "Tell the men to make it last. It's the only one we've got." It was a lie, but there was no point in risking someone rummaging through packs looking for more.

Hopefully a restful evening would keep the men's minds off the Indian they felt was refusing to do his job. Jefferson had overheard one of the men suggesting they string Brave Elk up for 'breeches a contacts'.

"Sumbitch! Look at that!" Smythe pointed back the way they had come. The elk with the broken antler had stopped, looking at them, in the middle of the path they had just blazed.

"Holy shit," Allman muttered incredulously.

The elk turned and began limping away. Before anyone could get a shot off, it moved out of sight. Allman and Bakker jumped back on their horses and started after it, closely followed by Smythe who was calling, "I sawed it first!"

Rutger pulled the cork from the bottle with his teeth, making a loud *pop*. "Go get 'em!" He growled encouragement and took a swig before offering the bottle to Hart.

Jefferson turned to look at Brave Elk. The Indian pointedly dismounted from his horse and headed for a clump of bushes, loosening his belt as he went.

It was dark when Crawley rode into camp, alone. The man was sullen and haggard looking. He ignored the calls from the men waving the whiskey bottle at him from the larger campfire and rode straight for Jefferson.

"Couldn't goddam wait for us? In a goddam hurry all of a sudden? Lost three men out there on accounta you!"

Jefferson stood from where he had been sitting with Brave Elk and faced Crawley.

"You and that goddam Injun," Crawley pointed angrily at Brave Elk, "think you can just wander off anyplace you goddam well feel like? You think—"

"That's quite enough, Mr. Crawley." Jefferson spoke in a low, quiet tone that almost couldn't be heard over Crawley's rant.

"I'll tell you when it's goddam enough!" Crawley drew his pistol, but Jefferson was faster. Crawley froze with his pistol half out, surprise widened his eyes.

"Contrary to your belief, Mr. Crawley, I am not unknowledgeable in the ways of the woods. I have spent nearly fifteen years walking across this great country and mapping it, like a civilized man, while you have grunted and scratched yourself like an animal, all the while claiming you know the land. I may not know this little piece of wilderness, but I know that you left with those men, and if you came back without them, then that's upon you. No one else."

Crawley eased his sidearm back into the holster. Anger burned deep in his eyes as they flicked from Jefferson to the Indian standing behind him.

Jefferson holstered his Colt without looking. "Those men are supposed to be competent enough to find their way in woods, or they wouldn't be here, but if you would like to regroup and go looking for them, you are welcome to it. However I recommend you wait until morning, as the only three men left in camp have been drinking."

Crawley turned to look over his shoulder at the fire where Rutger, Hart, and McKeely sat passing the bottle between themselves. "Where's the others?"

"They went after your elk, about three hours ago. Chased it back the way we came in."

"My elk?"

"Same elk. Broken antler, been shot."

Crawley snorted with disgust and turned his horse toward the three remaining men and their campfire.

"It has started," Brave Elk said softly.

Jefferson awoke at the cold of first light. He had not slept well. Every noise in the night brought thoughts of Crawley sneaking over to slit his throat in the darkness. He shook off the cold and rekindled the fire to brew coffee. Crawley and the other three men were still sleeping by the second campfire when Brave Elk walked into camp leading three horses, each with a body draped over it.

Crawley lurched to his feet at the sight of the Indian, gun in hand. "What'd you do to 'em?" he demanded. The other men roused up behind him, confused and disoriented.

Jefferson put down his coffee tin and picked up his gun belt, walking to the other campfire as Brave Elk ignored Crawley's bravado and walked back to the first horse.

Pushing up on the boots of the closest body, the Indian flipped the stiff form off the back of the horse, causing it to land face up with a sound thump. "Look into his face and you will see this is not the work of man."

Crawley stepped closer to see, gun still aimed at Brave Elk.

As Jefferson approached, he saw it was Mayer. The body's face was frozen in wide-open horror, showing the sickly brownish-yellow of the man's eyes and teeth. The skin had pinched tight as though Mayer had already been in the sun long enough for his body to bloat and contract again.

"Jesus H…" Crawley's gun barrel drifted off the Indian and to the ground, forgotten in his hand.

"What the hell?" Hart stepped forward to see around Rutger and McKeely. "He looks like one of them mummy things at the Freak Show."

Brave Elk pushed the bodies of Tamp and Dex off the horses, landing them hard on the ground. Their features wore the same petrified expression as Mayer. "If we do not turn back, we will all die." Brave Elk told Crawley. "The spirits did this. They do not want us here."

"Bullshit. You did this." Crawley raised his pistol and shot Brave Elk in the chest.

The Indian stumbled backward and fell, landing flat among the corpses.

Jefferson let his gun belt drop to the ground but his gun remained in his hand. He brought it up and leveled it at Crawley, nearly shaking with rage. "Drop it!"

Crawley looked at Jefferson and had the sense not to point his gun at him, but he didn't drop it. He kept it pointed down at Brave Elk, who had clasped one hand over his seeping wound and then stopped moving.

"Crawley. You drop that gun, or I'm going to drop you."

Rutger, McKeely, and Hart all waivered with hands near their holsters, not sure what to do.

"You gonna shoot me over an Injun?" Crawley's voice was full of disgust.

"I'm going to shoot you if you don't put that gun on the ground."

Crawley's eyes shifted to the other three men as he weighed his options. They all stood at the ready and Jefferson braced for the worst. Crawley slowly dropped the gun.

Keeping eyes on the others, Jefferson kept his gun on Crawley.

Crawley spat at Brave Elk's body before looking to Jefferson. "This is your fault."

"Get your gear and get out of here. You're dismissed, Mr. Crawley," Jefferson said.

They held eyes for a long moment. "You didn't hire me. The Railroad did."

"Nonetheless, I'm the one dismissing you. You *will* leave now."

Crawley narrowed his eyes and glared at Jefferson before his gaze went to the gun on the ground.

"Mr. Hart," Jefferson said without looking at the man, "would you be so kind as to store Mr. Crawley's weapon in his saddlebag for him?"

Hart didn't move.

A slight nod from Crawley finally put Hart in motion and the small man limped over to the gun and picked it up. Hart's eyes met

Crawley's again as he walked past him and he hesitated. Jefferson clenched his teeth as he held his gun steady and waited. After a moment, Hart turned and went to Crawley's bedroll, flipped open the saddlebag, and shoved the revolver into it.

"You ain't got no authority to dismiss me," Crawley repeated.

"I'd say pointing your gun at me last night and shooting my guide today is a good indication that you don't have a firm grasp of what your job was supposed to entail."

Crawley sneered and stepped forward, beginning to raise another objection, but Jefferson spoke over him and raised his weapon until it pointed at Crawley's face. "I've had enough of you, Mr. Crawley, and I know you've had enough of me. Let's let this end as peaceably as we can."

Crawley stopped, rage burning in his eyes. He turned his back on Jefferson, walked to his bedroll and pulled on his boots. Jefferson lowered the barrel of his gun, acutely aware Crawley could draw his gun from the saddlebag in a matter of seconds if he really wanted to. Crawley picked up his equipment and carried it to his mount. In a matter of moments he was sitting tall in his saddle.

He turned his horse and looked to Rutger, McKeely, and Hart. "You boys comin' with me to file complaint with the Railroad, or you stayin' here?"

The only three men left in Jefferson's expedition looked from Crawley to Jefferson and back again.

Rutger was the first to pick up his belongings and start for his horse. The other two followed quickly, Hart's limp only slowing him slightly.

They took the horses Brave Elk had brought with the bodies, and the supply mules—excepting Jefferson's personal mule—with them.

Waiting until the men had ridden far enough away that he could no longer see the disdain in their eyes, Jefferson went to Brave Elk. He stepped over the corpses to get to the Indian and kneeled down. Brave Elk winced at him with glassy eyes, but didn't move. Jefferson lifted Brave Elk's bloody hand, it came away from the wound it was covering with a sucking sound and Brave Elk began gasping for breath.

Jefferson put Brave Elk's hand back over the near perfectly round hole and the man's face became stoic again as he fought to breathe without breathing.

Looking up into the forest to see how far away Crawley, Rutger, McKeely, and Hart were, Jefferson was glad to note they were still moving away.

"I don't know what I can do for you, but I'll do what I can," he promised Brave Elk as he stood to get his small medical kit from the one remaining mule.

It was still well before noon when sounds in the forest changed and set the last two remaining horses nickering nervously. Jefferson had cleaned Brave Elk's wound as best he could, but found the man had problems breathing every time it was uncovered. He had finally used a piece of leather as a type of bandage and the Indian had finally drifted into unconsciousness.

Rising from Brave Elk's side, Jefferson turned and looked around the tree line surrounding what was left of the camp, searching for what had spooked the horses, but he saw nothing. Looking to the horses and mule, he saw which way their ears were cocked and focused his attention in that direction.

He expected Crawley to come back, but not so soon. Crawley seemed more like a slit your throat in the night person than one to attack in broad daylight.

The forest went dead silent. The heat of the day hadn't arrived to still the forest yet and Jefferson found the quiet out of place and unnerving. He slowly drew his pistol from its holster. This didn't feel like Crawley. This felt like the time he had been surrounded by a group of Indian warriors.

Jefferson held the pistol up for anyone to see and then laid it on the ground as far out as he could reach. He didn't want to appear a threat to an unknown tribe.

Shadows in the forest played tricks on his eyes. Was there movement?

A cracking branch, and then another, and Jefferson spotted a figure moving toward him through the brush and trees. It lurched and stumbled awkwardly.

Jefferson considered picking his gun up, but couldn't shake the feeling that eyes were on him.

Just as the figure was about to break far enough through the brush Jefferson could make it out, it stopped. A terrible scream filled the air. It came from the figure, yet also from all around the forest, causing the horses to startle and Jefferson to flinch and quickly turn around, but he saw nothing else.

The scream ran out of breath and the shape in the forest fell to the ground with a rustle of brush leaves and branches.

For what seemed like a long time, nothing moved and the world was silent. Then a bird chirped. Within moments the forest was alive again with the buzzing of insects and the wind gently blowing through the trees.

The figure was still barely visible to Jefferson. He turned and checked on Brave Elk. His eyes were closed and his breathing shallow. He didn't seem to have heard the scream.

Jefferson cautiously made his way to where he had last seen movement, intentionally leaving his gun behind. As he neared, he made out the shape of a man lying face down in the thick brush. The greasy hair was instantly recognizable as Smythe.

Rolling him over revealed the same permanent expression of terror and pinched skin the others had. Jefferson put the back of his hand to Smythe's cheek. It was icy cold and felt dried and papery, as though Smythe had died years ago and Jefferson had just found the body in the middle of a wintry blizzard.

Standing, Jefferson looked to see if there was anything else around. Either Smythe had just died right in front of him in some sort of God awful demonic way, or someone had brought his body here and made a show of it. In the direction Smythe would have been looking before he fell, Jefferson spotted a disturbance on the ground about fifty feet away.

Making his way over, he found a man's bare footprint. A print twice the size of any man's boot he'd ever seen.

❦

The bodies of Smythe, Mayer, Tamp and Dex were lying in a row, staring at the sky in terror, looking like a frozen portrait of the tortured souls Jefferson had once seen in an illustration of what Hell would be like.

He took his hat off and said a silent prayer over them. It

would have to do. He had no shovel, and even if he did, it would take him days to dig a grave for each of them.

And Brave Elk wouldn't last out here days.

The initial gunshot hadn't killed the Indian, nor had the long day or night following. Jefferson didn't know if the man would make it another day, a week, or die in the next ten minutes, but he wasn't going to sit around and find out. He was going to head back to the last area the expedition had seen people and hope someone could, or would, help the Indian.

He finished his prayer over the men he had come to think of as damned and then turned to the drag sled that had taken most of the evening and morning for him to make. The travois had given him something to work on by the fire as he sat vigil over Brave Elk all night. He couldn't have slept anyway. The footprint in the forest still haunted his thoughts. He'd been back to look at it several times, and it was still there every time he convinced himself he'd misidentified it.

Brave Elk, lying on the rigged stretcher attached to his horse, was pale but seemed in no immediate distress. Jefferson dribbled water into the man's mouth one more time in preparation for the trail. "I'm going to see if I can get you some help. You hang in there."

A close noise startled him and the horses. Turning, hand going for his gun, Jefferson expected to find Crawley and his men. Instead, he was surprised to see the elk with the broken antler, standing at the edge of the clearing, close enough to throw a rock at.

Jefferson let out a deep breath and took his hand off his pistol. He had no interest in shooting at the animal or following it to the fate that had befallen the other men. Turning away and ignoring it, he put the canteen away, mounted up, and grabbed the reins to the mule and Brave Elk's horse.

A thumping noise caught his attention, and Jefferson looked to see the elk pawing at the ground. When it saw him looking, the elk stood tall, with no sign of any limp or gunshot wounds, and started down a trail Jefferson hadn't noticed before. After a few steps, it turned and looked back.

Jefferson looked away and nudged his horse in the opposite direction.

The elk's bugle, while stridulating through high notes, reverberated through Jefferson's chest and seemed to shake the very earth beneath the horses' hooves. Jefferson looked back as the elk finished and it met his gaze. It lowered its head and pawed at the ground again, tearing up huge clumps of dirt. Then it turned and took steps down the path again, looking back at Jefferson.

Brave Elk moaned and shifted his head.

"All right," Jefferson said. "I can take a hint." He turned the horses to follow the elk down the path.

"Wait! Goddamnit! Wait!"

Before Jefferson could reach the path, Allman came stumbling out of the woods, blood running down his face from scratches and scrapes. His clothes were in tatters and his movements were wild and jerky. He kept his face pointed to the ground, never looking up at Jefferson.

Allman fell and then scrambled back to his feet. "It's one of them! It's a demon! Don't follow it!"

Shadows began moving in the forest around them, disappearing whenever Jefferson tried to look at them.

"Don't look at them!" Allman covered his eyes with his hands so that he could only see the ground in front of him. "They eat your soul! They suck it right out of your body!"

The forest grew darker with a presence Jefferson could feel but couldn't see. "Get on the horse," he called to Allman as he tried to control the increasingly spooked animals.

"We gotta go that way!" Allman pointed away from the elk and into what was increasingly the darkest part of the forest.

The elk bugled again. This time the sound had an urgent feel to it and Jefferson looked to see it trotting down the trail.

"Don't follow the demon!" Allman grabbed at the reins to Brave Elk's horse and tried to pull them from Jefferson's hand. "We have to go that way!"

The heaviness in the air grew oppressive and fear tingled across Jefferson's nerves as he noted the elk's trail seemed to be fading back into the forest. Allman pulled harder at the reins, but Jefferson refused to let go.

"Goddamn it!" Allman yelled and pulled his pistol. The hammer fell with an impotent *click* as he tried to shoot Jefferson.

"Hya!" Jefferson kicked his horse forward, nearly trampling

Allman and tearing control of the reins back. The horses needed little encouragement to escape the encroaching shadows wraithing through the trees. They reached the path just as Jefferson feared it would disappear.

The elk was far ahead, nearly out of sight. A scream filled the air, growing louder, and then Allman's body flew past Jefferson, landing to the side of the trail ahead.

The horses never slowed. Jefferson saw the man's face shriveling like a prune as they passed him, his scream drying up and dying in his throat as his eyes rolled back in terror.

And then the forest was gone.

The trail opened up into a wide, barren valley of dry red rocks like Jefferson had seen in the Badlands in the Utah Territory. The sun, still low on the morning horizon, was already hot and the air was nearly stagnant.

The horses slowed to a trot and then a walk. The elk was nowhere to be seen, but the valley, though wide, left little doubt about which way to go. Jefferson looked from the rocky cliffs to the clear sky and then over his shoulder back the way he'd come.

There was no sign of the dense, green California forest. The valley went on as far as he could see in both directions.

Brave Elk coughed and Jefferson stopped the horses and got down to give the man more water. He poured some in his palm and let each of the animals wet their mouths, and then he was out of water. He hadn't expected to be in the desert anytime soon, and even if he had, Crawley and his men had taken all of the other canteens.

The world began to turn orange and Jefferson looked up in surprise to see the sun was setting, not rising. Strange cries echoed from the cliffs as birds and bats began their evening feeding. Other shadows seemed to move among the rocks, and Jefferson felt eyes upon him, but they lacked the malicious feeling they'd had in the forest. Mostly.

Some of the shadows felt ominous as they slinked between boulders in his peripheral vision. Jefferson felt as though they were waiting for the light to leave so that they could get closer.

Glancing at the setting sun, he knew he had little time to build a fire to keep the darkness at bay. Looping the strap of the empty canteen on his saddle horn, he set about searching the dried land, trying to find anything that would burn. Brush was scarce and anything thicker than his little finger even scarcer. He found a dead cactus that he knew would light easily but would burn quick. The remains of larger bush, hidden behind a boulder that must have once provided shade and caught moisture, was his best find, but he knew it still wouldn't be enough fuel for more than an hour or so.

One last search of the area around his makeshift camp was all he had time for before the sun disappeared. When he returned, he spotted something lying next to Brave Elk. A piece of wood, nearly the size of his open hand. The biggest he'd seen out here. He bent to pick it up in the fading light and was startled to realize it wasn't wood.

It was a piece of broken antler.

Warm in his hand, it fit his palm perfectly, like a tool crafted just for him. He looked down to Brave Elk. The man didn't look as though he had moved since Jefferson had given him water, and Jefferson was pretty sure he would have noticed if Brave Elk had had the antler on him when tending his wound.

Then the dark was upon them. Jefferson hooked the antler piece in his belt and began tending the tiny fire. Made of twigs, it hardly put out enough light to reflect in the horses' eyes. Jefferson struggled to see in the starlight as he unsaddled the horses and dug through packs. He did his best to wrap Brave Elk in a blanket, leaving him on the litter but lowering it from his horse, and then settled down beside him.

The red eyes glowing in the dark were too big, too wide set, to be natural, and they made Jefferson's throat constrict with fear. They were the forward facing eyes of a predator.

Jefferson drew his pistol and waited.

More eyes appeared, shining with unnatural light that was not the reflection of the fire or the stars, surrounding the camp. The horses began pacing nervously.

Something moved quickly behind him, and Jefferson spun, gun ready, but whatever it was, it was already gone. Another movement behind him, and another, each time he turned, something behind him.

They were working together, trying to wear him down.

He leveled his gun and aimed between the eyes in front of him. They stared back, unblinking, watching intently, as if daring him to fire. A quiet movement came from behind him and he lowered his gun and cautiously turned around.

He had to look up three feet to meet the creature's eyes.

There was an intelligence in the eyes. Angry, disapproving, but intelligence nonetheless.

The stories so many peoples had told him of the Giants flooded his mind. He had dismissed them all, and yet, here now stood one before him. A man, but not a man, easily twice the size of most men, covered in fur like a bear, held out an enormous hand, palm up, and glared into Jefferson's eyes.

Swallowing hard, Jefferson handed over his weapon. It would be no use against even one of these creatures anyway.

With a face wrinkled in disgust, the creature tossed the weapon to the ground and held out its hand again.

Heart racing, Jefferson didn't know what to do, only that he was at this thing's mercy. Brave Elk groaned. Jefferson's eyes flicked from the Indian to the eyes of the thing, and he finally understood.

He took the piece of broken antler from where he had hooked it to his belt and handed it to the Giant, to the keeper of this world that man had been exiled from.

The creature grunted as the antler vanished into its palm. The other eyes in the darkness disappeared as the giant turned and strode into the darkness.

Jefferson found himself staring at the enormous footprints long after the creature was gone.

The grass tickling Jefferson's nose woke him with a start. He sat up and blinked at the sun high in the blue sky. Rolling green hills surrounded him and the grazing horses. Brave Elk still lie on the travois next to him, breathing quietly. Voices in the distance caught his attention and stood to see approaching horses.

Squinting at them, Jefferson was amazed when he realized he was looking at people from Brave Elk's tribe. One of them raised a hand in recognition and he returned the gesture, grateful for a friendly face.

Crawley stomped into the Railroad office with Hart, McKeely, and Rutger close behind. "We're here to file complaint," he said before the man behind the counter had even looked up.

"Names?" the man, who wore a round cap and uniform jacket with polished brass in spite of being indoors, asked as he looked up at them over tiny oval glasses.

"Crawley, Hart, Rutger, and McKeely," Crawley barked. "We're here to file complaint against—"

"Oh!" The station master looked up surprised, interrupting Crawley. "These are for you." He read each man's name from an envelope and passed them out as they acknowledged who they were.

The men tore the envelopes open and pulled out letters before looking at each other, confused.

"It ain't pay," McKeely said.

"What is this?" Crawley demanded.

"Letters of dismissal." The man pushed his glasses up on his nose as he looked at the men. "Mr. Jonathon Thomas Jefferson was in three days ago and filed notice of your terminations for abandoning your duties."

"Three days ago!" Hart stammered. "That was a five day ride!"

"And he was at least a day behind us!" McKeely added.

Crawley punched McKeely in the arm. "Shut up!" He turned back to the station master. "We are still filing complaint against Jefferson! He had no right or authority to dismiss us!"

"Actually," a voice came from behind them, "he had every right."

The four men turned to find a man with a badge on his chest standing in the doorway. "Shooting an unarmed man in the chest with intent to kill him in cold blood is a hanging offence."

"He weren't no man! He was a goddamned Indian!" Crawley growled, fists clenched.

"He was under employment of the Railroad," the sheriff said. "That changes things a bit. Not to mention, the report filed for your arrest mentions the death of five other men, and one more missing, while under your watch."

"That was Jefferson's fault!"

"Nonetheless, Mr. Crawley, you are under arrest. You will have your chance to explain it all to the judge. "

Crawley ground his teeth and turned red as the sheriff handcuffed him.

"Are *we* under arrest?" Rutger pulled nervously at his red beard.

"Did you do anything wrong?" the sheriff asked, eyeing the other three men.

"Uh…" Hart seemed to think hard on the question. McKeely found an interesting spot on the toe of his boot.

The sheriff smiled. "Why don't you come down to the jail, friendly-like, and we'll see if your side of the story matches that of Mr. Jefferson and Brave Elk?"

## Colorado 1895

Looks to be a killin' snow," Joel commented as he looked out over the wet rocks and dripping pine trees dotting the hill around them. Fat, wet flakes slapped him on the cheek and stuck to his eyelashes. He gave his older brother a worried glance. If they got wet and temperatures dropped below freezing, they would be in trouble. The top of Harold's hat was already soaked with white splotches impacting and melting, and his horse's mane was matting with the damp.

Joel reached over the side of his saddle and wiped the wet off of the stock of his old Henry Rifle. As he dug out the holster cover and tied it off to protect the rifle, Harold finally answered.

"I was thinking the same. We should head back. Which way you reckon is fastest? Back the way we came, or over through Turtle Gulch?" Harold followed Joel's example and closed the flap on his own rifle holster, protecting the newer Winchester he'd gotten for his fifteenth birthday, two months earlier.

Joel was glad his brother had agreed so readily, he didn't want to seem like a child on their first hunting trip out without their father. He was nearly thirteen, but he still felt like the baby of the family. Not to mention they hadn't brought winter gear for an overnight hunt, and even if they had, a night under a layer of ice was a miserable thing.

"I'm thinking this is coming down pretty hard." Joel looked up into the gray sky, blinking at the flakes bouncing off his face as he considered his brother's question. "Turtle Gulch might be running wet soon. 'Til it freezes, anyways. I say we go back, avoid the water, even if it is farther."

"Sound thought." Harold approved.

Joel turned his horse around and headed back along the game trail they had followed on the way in. The click of the horses' hooves on the rocks seemed louder now that the snow dampened the sounds of the forest around them. Silence hung between the brothers, a reminder their hunt had failed.

Joel tried not to feel miserable, but the hunt had already felt strange without their father along. It had felt...lonely. He trusted Harold, and he thought he could even trust himself alone out here in the mountains, but there was some small fear, way down deep inside, that he couldn't shake without his father's presence.

Their horses' ears twitched and perked forward as an animal bleated from somewhere ahead.

Harold raised his eyebrows and looked at Joel questioningly as they listened.

"Sounds like a fawn," Joel whispered. "Isn't it too late in the year?"

Harold frowned at the sound drifting down through the snow and the trees again. It was a plaintive, high-pitched cry, almost a squeal.

"Sounds young," Harold agreed and nudged his horse on forward toward the sound, moving ahead of Joel.

As they approached the bleating sound, Joel spotted movement up the hill. He clicked his tongue to get Harold's attention and then pointed. They both slowed their horses and kept watch upslope as falling snow streaked across their field of view.

A small fawn stumbled into view on ungainly legs, stopping to cry again before clumsily hopping behind a brush pile.

Joel reined in his horse and looked at Harold, confusion on his face. "That fawn can't be more'n a week old."

The birthing season had ended five to six months ago.

Harold nodded. "It won't survive the night. Not in this weather," Harold muttered. The wet snow had nearly drenched both of them and showed no signs of stopping. "There's probably a momma close around here somewhere, too. You wanna look for it, or head on home?"

Normally they would leave a fawn and its mother alone. This late in the year though, a fawn that young didn't stand a chance of surviving the winter anyway. Joel wiped a drip of water from his nose, considered the damp chill, and looked around. The snow was starting to stick to the ground and seemed to be coming down harder by the minute.

Harold must have seen the discomfort on his face. "Let's go home. It's getting cold," he said.

Relieved, Joel urged his mount on to follow his brother. The horses' footing became unsure as the ground turned muddy and slick. The fawn's cry increased as they moved on, seeming to follow them, as if, up on the hill, the fawn was pacing them. They both kept eyes in the directions of the sounds as they moved.

"What's that?" Joel pointed at a large dark spot behind the trees above them. "Is that a cave?"

Harold squinted at it. "It sure looks like it."

"Wanna go check it out?" Joel couldn't keep the excitement out of his voice. He hadn't ever seen a cave big enough to go into before.

"Nope." Harold shook his head. "But we've been by here a hundred times and never seen it afore. If we don't go now, like as not, we'll never see it again. Let's be quick, I don't like this weather." He turned his horse upslope and prodded it on.

Joel followed, more excited than he had been when he found out they would get to go hunting on their own. As the cave loomed before them, he couldn't understand how they hadn't ever seen it before. It was big enough for them to ride into side by side, if the opening were only a little taller.

Joel looked over his shoulder at his brother. "Maybe a warm place to stay the night, keep out of the snow 'til it stops."

The fawn squealed, running out from a nearby bush, startling the horses and the boys. Wobbly legs shaking, it disappeared into the dark of the cave opening,

Harold grinned at Joel, obviously shaking off a case of the nerves. "A little Bed and Breakfast?"

Joel grinned back, glad he wasn't the only one who had been caught off guard. He dismounted and drew his Colt.

"I'd stick with your Henry, if I was you. Might be something big in there."

Joel nodded nervously, holstered his pistol, and handed his reigns to Harold. He untied the holster cover and pulled out his rifle. With a backwards glance over his shoulder, he walked into the mouth of the cave, his head clearing the rocky overhang with ease. The dark swallowed him quickly and he stood for a moment trying to let his eyes adjust. White spots on the ground ahead slowly appeared as his vision improved.

"How far's it go?" Harold asked from outside.

"Can't tell. Looks like a long ways," Joel answered as he moved deeper in, trying to get a look at the white areas on the floor. He toed one and it rattled like a pile of dried sticks. Bending down to feel, he recognized the texture in his hands. "There's lots of old bones in here," he called back, forgetting he might scare the fawn out. "Lots of 'em."

"Is there room enough to bring the horses in out of the snow?"

Joel looked around, trying to make out the walls. "I think so. We need to make a light. I can't see anything!" He turned to head back to the opening.

The fawn's lamenting cry came from deeper down in the cave, startling him. He looked but couldn't see anything. He needed more light. As he left the cave, the squealing reached a near-fever pitch.

"That thing sounds hurt. Must've caught its leg or something in there," Harold commented as Joel came back out into the snow.

"It's just too dark in there." Joel dug into his pack for matches and headed into the trees to find kindling. When he got back with an armful, Harold had made a fire pit inside the cave, just as far as he could go in and still see. The fawn was still calling for its mother from the darkness below.

"Thing is enough to start to make you crazy!" Harold told him. "Can't imagine trying to stay the night with that noise."

"Pretty sure were stayin'." Joel pointed back outside where the snow was already over an inch deep in places.

Harold frowned. "Get that fire lit. I'll bring the horses in here. See if we can get them dry."

Joel struggled with the damp kindling as he watched Harold try to coax the horses into the cave. Both animals were disturbed by the constant bleating coming from below.

When the warm light of the fire finally filled the darkness, Joel felt as though a pressure had been lifted off him. He stood and looked back into the darkness. The flickering light now revealed at least a dozen piles of old bones, more than he had originally thought. Examining the closest few, he called out to Harold.

"Look at this! These are bear, and this one's mountain lion, and that one over there looks like wolf!"

Harold finished tying off the horses inside the cave and came to see.

"All of these are predators. Every last one," Joel said from further down in. "Isn't that queer?"

"It is," Harold agreed. "You'd think we'd be finding the bones of the kills, not the killers. Come on, we need to get more wood for the fire, before it's all buried in the snow."

Joel looked back into the dark where the squealing had quieted some.

"I don't think it's going anywhere, and we need wood. Come on."

Joel followed Harold out into the gray daylight, fighting the urge to duck under the overhang as he came out. The fawn's squalling picked up again as they exited.

Harold shook his head at the noise and ignored it. "I'll look over here, you head that way. Don't go too far. It's easy to get turned around in the snow."

"I can follow my tracks back," Joel assured him.

"This snow'll fill your tracks in minutes," Harold admonished and set out away from his brother.

* * *

The warmth of the fire was lost in the cool of the cave as Joel entered, ducking to avoid hitting his head on the overhang, but at least it was dry and out of the wind and snow. He added his load to the pile of wood stacked to the side of the fire. It was more than enough to get them through the night now. The cries of the fawn from below had quieted and only came intermittently now, making the sound much more bearable.

"Okay." Harold nodded at Joel. "Let's go see if we can find dinner."

"Should I bring the rifle? Or just the Colt?"

Harold pointed at the bone piles around them. "I don't want to be shooting no bear with a pea-shooter, you?"

139

Joel shook his head and picked up his rifle from where he had laid it out to dry. He stooped and picked up the small storm lantern they had lit. He looked back at Harold. "I can't carry the lamp and shoot a rifle both. Maybe I ought to just carry the Colt, let you bring a rifle."

Harold nodded approvingly and grabbed his rifle.

"You remember hearing about that Windy Cave or whatever?" Joel asked as they started stepping around the bones. "Down by Manitou? That guy was charging people money to go in his cave! You think we could do that?"

Harold stopped and looked around at the plain brown walls. "I don't know why anyone would pay good money to look at a big hole in the ground."

The fawn bleated again, this time closer. Joel held the lantern higher, trying to send the light farther into the darkness sloping away downwards in front of them. "I think it splits off ahead."

As they got closer, two dark tunnels became apparent. The distress calls from the young deer came from the one on the left.

Joel looked to Harold, who pointed to the left.

More bone piles littered the floor; many of them scattered and mixed in with others. As they moved deeper, the tunnel curved to the right, eventually becoming a hard enough turn they were unable to see around the bend. The bleats stayed ahead of them, somehow never getting louder. Then the tunnel opened up again, with a smaller tunnel leading off to the right. The cries finally seemed louder now, coming from the smaller tunnel.

Joel started towards the sounds.

"Hold up," Harold called from behind him. "Bring that light back here."

"What is it?" Joel asked even as he saw for himself. Tracks led in from the wider area and down the tunnel Joel had been headed for. Human tracks.

Harold stepped up and planted his boot next to one of the prints, then pulled it away. It was a perfect match.

"Those are our tracks?" Joel stepped next to the other set and pulled his foot away. The boot prints matched. "We were walking in a circle. Why didn't we see the fawn? Is it moving ahead of us? Where's its tracks?"

"I don't like this," Harold muttered. "This doesn't feel good." He looked down the tunnel where the cries came from, and then back up the way their tracks had come from. "We need to get out of here."

Joel hesitated, listening to the fawn. It was so close now he couldn't believe they couldn't see it.

"Joel. Go."

Joel started back, following their tracks. The sound of the cry changed, it became a more desperate, wounded cry, as if the fawn was not only lost, but severely injured. A smell washed over Joel. Blood. Warm and pungent in the air.

"You smell that? It smells like a fresh kill."

"Keep going. I think this is a bad place. We need out."

One of the horses screamed ahead of them, and Harold broke into a trot, passing Joel. "Come on!"

As they ascended, they spotted the glow of the campfire lighting the walls and the horses before they saw the fire itself. The horses had pulled free of their loose tethers and backed farther into the cave, past the campfire, facing out. Outside the cave, darkness had come early with the snow.

"Wolves!" Joel cried out as he heard the snarling and saw dark shapes moving outside the cave.

"Try to get the horses under control," Harold directed, "I'll scare the wolves off."

Joel approached the horses from a wide angle, so they would recognize him. He called reassuringly to them and caught their reigns as his brother knelt next to the campfire and aimed his rifle. The distinctive clicking sound echoed in the cave as he worked the Winchester's lever to chamber a cartridge.

"You got 'em?"

"Got 'em!" Joel called.

Harold's rifle cracked, deafeningly loud in the cave. The darkness outside hid any reaction to the gunfire, but the snarling continued as dark shapes moved. Harold worked the lever and fired again, and again, with no visible reaction.

Joel kept the reigns tight as the horses nervously pawed at the ground, unwilling to move farther back into the darkness towards the smell of blood and the sound of the squealing fawn, yet afraid of the wolves outside the cave.

Harold fired again. "I can't hit any of them!" He stood up and drew his pistol, walking towards the mouth of the cave.

"Why aren't they scared off?" Joel heard the panic in his own voice and worried that his brother would hear it too.

"I think I have an idea," Harold called back and stepped out of the light of the campfire, ducking low to avoid the overhanging entrance. The snarling increased in intensity.

"Harry? Harry, are you all right?"

After a long moment of listening to the snarling wolves, Joel finally heard his brother reply.

"I'm fine! Come here!"

Joel dropped the reigns and patted the horses, trying to reassure them. He drew his own pistol and picked up the lantern. He bumped his head on the overhang, knocking his hat off as he moved out of the cave and into the night. Holding the lamp high, Joel lit up as much area as he could.

"What do you see?" Harold asked.

Joel looked into the gloom. "Nothing." He could still hear the growls in the trees. "Just…movement."

"Exactly. There's no eye shine. And no tracks." He pointed at the ground. "I don't think there's any wolves out here any more than there was a fawn in there. Something queer is going on here. Let's get back to the horses."

Joel followed Harold back, stopping to pick up his hat as he ducked back under the overhanging entrance, careful not to hit his head this time. As he placed the hat back on his head, he stopped to look at the overhang.

"Harry?"

"Yeah?"

"The horses didn't have to duck when you walked them in…did they?"

"Whaddya mean?" Harold turned to look back at his brother.

Joel pointed up at the cave opening. "I think this used to be bigger."

Harold walked back over and stood next to Joel, looking at his brother, then at the opening. "Jesus, Mary, and Joseph. Get our stuff. We gotta get out of here. I'll get the horses, you get our gear!"

Joel grabbed at the blankets and saddles that had been sat to dry near the fire and carried them out into the snow while Harold struggled with pulling the horses towards the sounds of angry wolves. The horses fought, refusing to go.

Joel came back in, panic in his voice. "What do we do? I'm not even sure they can fit back out, it's getting smaller!"

Harold cursed as he gave up and let go of the reigns, watching the horses move past the fire and back into the darkness of the cave. "Forget the horses. *We* gotta get out." He kicked the pile of firewood in frustration.

"What's going on? I don't understand."

"Look around, Joel! There was no deer, there are no wolves. This cave eats things! It lures them in and closes down its mouth and eats them!" He waved his arms in frustration. "It's too late to save the horses. We gotta get out."

"It's alive?" Joel looked around the cave wide-eyed, fear in his voice.

"Come on. Let's get out before it closes."

"Wait! If it eats, it's gotta be alive, right? And if it's alive, we can kill it."

"How? Dig a hole in it? You got a pick? I don't."

"Maybe we can hurt it!" Joel grabbed an armful of firewood and carried it to the shrinking opening. He laid it out under the overhang and went back for more.

"You thinking it'll burn?"

"Maybe enough to open its mouth so we can get the horses out. What have we got to lose?"

"You mean besides our lives, if we don't get out of here?" Harold sighed and helped move the last of the wood over, then they grabbed the burning pieces out of the campfire and lit the pile.

"All right. Outside. We don't want to be in here if this don't work."

They stood next to the fire to keep warm and watched as the opening continued to come closer to the ground. The movement was imperceptibly slow, but undeniable real as the overhang moved slowly closer to the fire. The snarling sounds from behind them continued in the dark, sometimes sounding closer, sometimes more vicious, but never did any wolf show more than a moving shadow.

"What are we gonna tell Pa?" Joel worried what Pa was going to say when he came back from their first hunt without the horses.

"You leave Pa to me. I'll tell him straight." Harold stomped his feet to make a place to stand in the knee-deep snow. "Gonna be a long, cold night. At least we had a chance to get dry in there. We won't freeze to death tonight. Hell, as long as we got a fire like this going, we ought to just have ourselves a bonfire. Keep good and warm all night. Bring that lantern, let's see how much wood we can find."

"What about the wolves?"

"If there's a real wolf out here, my name's Winchester."

They gathered everything they could find and piled it on the fire. Harold found a half-rotted log, and together they rolled and dragged it into the fire.

The fire was roaring big as any fire Joel had ever seen when they felt the ground shake. The horses whinnied from inside the cave, and he dropped to a knee to see inside. They had moved closer to the entrance, now that the sounds of wolves had stopped coming from the forest. One of the horses reared up, eyes rolling, and moved closer to the entrance, avoiding the side with the fire.

Over the crackle of the fire and the sounds of the horses, he could hear snarling again, this time from the back of the cave.

"You hear that, Harry?"

A smirk pulled at Harold's lips. "Your idea must be working. It wants us out, instead of in, now."

"I think you're right. I think the opening is getting bigger! We may get the horses back after all."

Joel watched as Pa looked over the blackened rocks of the overhang, just above his head. "Must've been a hell of a fire you boys built, to toss soot up this high."

"No, Pa. Those rocks was only this high off the ground when the fire was hittin' 'em." Harold held his hand out at knee height. "They moved."

"Rocks don't move, son. Not uphill, anyways."

"I think we killed it," Joel told him. "It never moved again after that third time the whole ground shook and those trees up there fell over."

"Eh!" Pa dismissed him. "Wet ground and heavy snows. You boys oughta stayed in the cave. Lucky you didn't get killed in a landslide."

Joel turned away, disgusted. He'd told Harold that Pa wouldn't believe them.

A squeaking sound caught his ear and he followed it, glad for the distraction. He tracked the sound to a bush. As he reached down to move it aside, a baby mouse, still hairless, squealed and ran into a hole no bigger than a silver dollar.

He stood up and started to walk away. The squeaking continued. He looked back just in time to see the baby mouse run back into the hole again.

"Harry! Come see this! It's a baby cave monster!"

A Colorado native, Sam Knight spent ten years in California's wine country before returning to the Rockies. When asked if he misses California, he gets a wistful look in his eyes and replies he misses the green mountains in the winter, but he is glad to be back home.

As well as being Distribution Manager for WordFire Press, Sam is Senior Editor for Villainous Press and author of five children's books, four short story collections, two novels, and nearly three dozen short stories, including two media tie-ins co-authored with Kevin J. Anderson: Wayward Pines: Aberration (Kindle Worlds, 2014) and Of Monsters and Men, Planet of the Apes: Tales from the Forbidden Zone (Titan, 2016).

A stay-at-home father, Sam attempts to be a full-time writer, but there are only so many hours left in a day after kids. Once upon a time, he was known to quote books the way some people quote movies, but now he claims having a family has made him forgetful, as a survival adaptation. He can be found at SamKnight.com and contacted at Sam@samknight.com

Rhye Manhattan is a rather reclusive and private author, and Sam was excited to have had the fortune to collaborate with her on *Moshito Masquine* and hopes to do so again in the future. (They have discussed a couple of stories…)